My Abandonment

Peter Rock was born and raised in Salt Lake City. *My Abandonment* won an Alex Award, the Utah Book Award, and has been published in various countries and languages. He has taught fiction at the University of Pennsylvania, Yale, Deep Springs College, and in the MFA program at San Francisco State University. His stories and freelance writing have both appeared and been anthologised widely. The recipient of a National Endowment for the Arts Fellowship and other awards, he currently lives in Portland, Oregon, where he teaches writing.

My Abandonment

PETER ROCK

JOHN MURRAY

First published in the United States of America in 2010 by Mariner Books,
Houghton Mifflin Harcourt

First published in Great Britain in 2018 by John Murray (Publishers)
An Hachette UK Company

I

© Peter Rock 2009, 2008

Portions of this work were previously published in *Tin House*, volume 9, number 3, 2008.

A CIP catalogue record for this title is available from the British Library

ISBN 978-1-473-69196-4
Ebook ISBN 978-1-473-69197-1

Designed by Lydia D'moch

Printed and bound in Great Britain by Clays Ltd, Elcograf S.p.A.

John Murray policy is to use papers that are natural, renewable and recyclable
products and made from wood grown in sustainable forests. The logging and
manufacturing processes are expected to conform to the environmental
regulations of the country of origin.

John Murray (Publishers)
Carmelite House
50 Victoria Embankment
London EC4Y ODZ

www.johnmurray.co.uk

For Ida Akiko Rock

It is remarkable how many creatures live wild and free though secret in the woods, and still sustain themselves in the neighborhood of towns, suspected by hunters only.

—Henry David Thoreau, *Walden*

Very soon after, I saw a little snake. He was crawling along. When I see snakes, I like to stop and watch. The dresses they wear fit them tight—they can't fluff out their clothes like birds can. But snakes are quick people. They move in such a pretty way. Their eyes are bright, and their tongues are slim.

—Opal Whiteley,
The Singing Creek Where the Willows Grow

One

Sometimes you're walking through the woods when a stick leaps into the air and strikes you across the back and shoulders several times, then flies away lost in the underbrush. There's nothing to do but keep walking, you have to be ready for everything and I am as I follow behind Father down out of the trees, around a puddle, to the fence of the salvage yard. It's night.

"Caroline," Father says, holding open a tear in the fence. "You come through here."

He begins to sort and scavenge. He wants rebar, metal to support our roof. I watch the road, the gate and also behind us where we came through. Cars and big trucks rush and rattle past on the highway, the people inside staring straight ahead and thinking about where they are going and what will happen next and probably things they've done before but they're not thinking of or looking at us. There are no houses near the salvage yard. An electrical station humming inside its own fences and then on the other side Fat Cobra Video, which Father says is a snake store but I don't think it is. In the window are pictures of ladies with their shirts off, holding their breasts in their hands.

Now he is pulling out the long thin metal bars, setting the scraps of sheet metal aside. I hold Randy, my toy horse, in one hand. If I set him down it's never for long. Randy and my blue piece of ribbon are always with me.

"You see, Caroline," Father says, "all the work I'm doing here for these people, organizing all these different things. This is how we are paying them back for what we're taking."

"Yes," I say, squinting across the highway to the dark trains in the railyard, the tiny lights of the cars on the bridge over the river.

The rebar and wire are happy to be with us since we will put them to better use and not forget them to rust in a pile. Father bends back the fence so you'd never know we were here. In one hand I carry a roll of wire that will help hold up the roof or which we can bend to a hanging shelf or another secret thing he might make and in my other hand is Randy softly rattling with the things I put inside his hollow body. My finger is over the round hole in his stomach.

"Caroline, don't lag."

"I'm right here," I say.

Father keeps backtracking since it's hard to carry the long pieces of rebar through the trees in the dark. They keep snagging on things, turning him sideways.

"If you look up at the sky," I say, "you can see the spaces between the trees that way and see where to walk."

"Thanks," he says. "Who do you think taught you that?"

At night the air smells less dry, the coolness in the trees. A branch clatters down, becoming a stick. Squirrels up there? An owl? Everything in the darkness reaches out, in its way and at night we wear shoes so it's harder to feel how things are. We go deeper into the forest park, further from the edge where the city leans in. I know where we are. I know the way home and where I would end up if I walked thirty minutes in any direction through the forest. If I hold my breath and let Father walk away I can't even hear his footsteps, even in his shoes. That's how good he is.

Then the air is thick and rotten. Father's hand is on my arm. I hear the click and then his headlamp is bright and round on his forehead. He holds back a tangle of blackberry and I step through and on the ground is a deer with its neck bent back and its eyes missing and blood on its black nose. The light is a five inch white circle sliding across the deer. Its head, its hooves, its tail. The deer is about the size of me, its tan fur smooth, flies bouncing and buzzing. Its stomach is open and some parts are missing.

"That's her liver," Father says, pointing with a stick, sharp black against the light. "Lungs. Heart."

"The dogs did this?" I say. "The smell."

"Hold your breath," Father says. "I doubt it was dogs, or coyotes. Someone might have shot her, or disease, or she could have even fallen down here and broken her neck. Even animals can fall down sometimes."

"I know that," I say.

"Look carefully, Caroline. There's a lesson here. It's better homework than being in school, that's for certain."

Father turns his neck to look at me before I can shut my eyes against the brightness and it blinds me. I hear the switch so I know it's off but still the light is in my eyes and they take a moment to clear and we can walk again.

A little further on Father stops at a good place where it is finally not so steep and sets everything down. He pulls up the ivy around and over it even though almost no one would come here or find or want or be able to carry it.

"There," he says. "We've done it again, Caroline."

We step only on the stones, closer to home. I on every one, Father on every second one. To not beat down the grass. We come around the side and carefully he takes away the branch across the front door and then we sit on the edge of the mattress for a moment before he strikes a match and lights the lamp. The lamp is made out of a glass bottle with fuel in it and a string stuck through into it. Its light shines and deeper back in the cave the gold letters on my encyclopedias shine back. I only have up to L but I haven't read past E. I go into F or G or the future ones when something's mentioned that starts with that letter. My dictionary is there, too. It is a paperback book and smaller.

Inside the ceiling is tall enough that I can stand on my knees but Father has to sit down or crawl. He pulls the branch back across the door and looks at me.

"We're lucky," he says. "We're the lucky ones."

"We are," I say.

"We have to be so careful these days," he says.

"Why?"

"People."

"No one knows where we are," I say.

"If you think that way," Father says, "that's when you get caught. Overconfident."

"No one's ever caught us," I say. "No one could."

"That doesn't mean anything," he says. "You know better than to look to the past, Caroline."

I set Randy on his wooden base with the one metal post the size of a pencil that fits in the hole in his stomach. I turn his white side out so I can look up and check on him in the darkness and he'll be easy to see from the mattress.

The dinner dishes are all dry now and I stack them on their shelves. Father takes off his dark forest pants and mends a rip with a piece of dental floss and a needle. Then he writes down things from the books he's reading in his tiny handwriting in his little book and I do some homework he's given me and I also write on the scrap paper some of this journal and things I've seen and thought. Father, his hand spread out is wider than this sheet of paper, wider than the plates we eat off, his fingertips hanging over. It makes a book look tiny when he holds it.

We brush our teeth and spit in the chamber pot and change out of our clothes and lie down on the mattress. Father stretches his hands over his head so they almost reach the flat stone and the green Coleman stove. Sometimes in his sleep his hands cross and his wrists come together and his bracelets ring softly. They're supposed to help him be stronger. When I tell him I need help to be stronger, he says that I haven't seen all the things or had the problems he's had. He says I'm too young to wear jewelry. He turns over to kiss me, his scratchy cheek.

IF A PARAGRAPH is a thought, a complete thought, then a sentence is one piece of a thought. Like in addition where one number plus another number equals a bigger number. If you wrote down subtraction you would start with a thought and take enough away that it was no longer complete. You might write backward, or nothing at all, or less than nothing. You wouldn't even think or breathe. A comma, that is a place you breathe, or think, which is how breathing and thinking are the same. They collect, or are places to collect. A semicolon is a strange kind of thinking that I don't understand. It is more than one sentence inside one sentence. It makes more sense to me just to let each sentence be a sentence. Father says both the pieces on either side of a colon should add up to the same thing, even if one side is just a list. Some of the things I need to write about: Randy, the look-outs, bodies, names, Nameless, people when they think they're alone, snow, trampolines, helicopters.

"WAKE UP," I say. "You were having a dream. Was it the helicopters?"

"Whoa," Father says. "I guess it was a dream."

"I can't see the moon," I say. "It's dark outside tonight."

"Clouds," he says. "Maybe it'll rain tomorrow."

"Was it the helicopters?"

"Oh Caroline," he says. "They swarmed all down over the trees, rattling and tearing at everything. They had loudspeakers and from above they cast the sound of a baby crying, so loud, crying, the edges breaking up."

"Why? This was in your dream?"

"No, this was before. I don't know."

"Why would they do that?" I say.

"Exactly. I don't know. Sleep, Caroline."

In the summer like now we sleep on top of the sleeping bags with only a sheet over us and in the winter we zip the bags together since it's warmer that way. When my body was smaller there was lots of room but now even when it's too warm I cannot get away, our legs touch, our arms. I can't fall asleep and I can't tell if Father is asleep or not. I keep thinking of the deer, dead, lying half a mile away, listening while different animals drag parts of her away. Father does not grow but he is the largest man in the forest park that I have seen, bigger than anyone in the city except very fat men who cannot move like he moves. I am also quick but much more slender and five feet tall, my dark hair long and snarled and my skin white so it can flash in a darkness if I'm not careful.

All at once there's a whining, a snarling and then a snuffling as a snout pushes through the branch across our door. It's the dogs, some of them, racing through our camp, and Father shouts once and bangs a pan with a spoon and they're gone that fast but I know that he's awake.

"I named the head dog Lala," I say.

"If she's such a good friend of yours," he says, "you could tell her that we try to sleep around here at night."

"I was thinking about the deer," I say. "The dead one."

"What about her?"

"Nothing," I say, the bottoms of my feet on his leg. "What is your favorite color?"

"What's yours?"

"Yellow," I say.

"Why?"

"The way it makes me feel. It's bright and not still."

"Exactly. It draws attention. I like green."

"You would," I say, and he laughs and holds me close.

"And what was my mother's favorite color?"

"Yellow. Just like yours."

"So she taught me that, for it to be my favorite."

"Probably," he says. "Kind of, some way. You're very much like her."

"And we have the same name."

"Had," he says. "Yes. Caroline."

"Why did you give me the same name?"

"Because I loved her so much. Now go to sleep; it's the middle of the night, Caroline. I always tell you that."

"I wish I could have met her."

"She wishes that, too," he says. "Good night, yellow."

"Good night, green."

SINCE I AM THIRTEEN I am allowed to get out of bed whenever I wake up. Even before the sun, like now. Father sleeps on his stomach with his face in the pillow and his arms stretched out underneath it, his big hands on the ground. If he sleeps on his back he snores and I have to wake and tell him so he'll turn over in the night since snoring is a sound.

The zipper is cold but the morning is not too cold. I pull on my black jeans and my dark green sweatshirt over my nightshirt and I get Randy off his stand and leave him with his horse's head on my pillow, safe in the bed with Father. I take the chamber pot I used once last night and the water bucket and I slip out not knocking the branch over, the branch that goes across the door when we're not here and sometimes when we're sleeping. In the winter we hang a wool blanket across, inside, to hold in the heat of our bodies.

The bugs are already up in the warm air and I only need my two shirts. Father says now I have to wear an undershirt under my other shirt even if my breasts are almost flat. In the winter I wear sweaters and a dark raincoat. At the men's camp people wear garbage bags with arm and head holes torn out but Father says that is not right. I also in the winter wear tights beneath my jeans. Father wears waffled long underwear all year around. The legs are gray and the top is red. He wears a dark plaid shirt that smells like wool and him, his hair and everything.

I hop across the stones and walk out under the trees, past my hidden garden. The lettuce is easy, even if it's hard to clean. The beans want more sun than they get and I am impatient and dig up the radishes before they're ready.

A chipmunk darts quicker than a squirrel but a squirrel's more aware, his head jerking around from side to side, perched on a branch. Squirrels fall sometimes even if watching them it seems impossible.

Little maples try to grow up through the ivy that Father hates. The ground is all steep and rough and sometimes I'm hardly thinking as I go and then sometimes inside I'm saying Quiet, Caroline. Look at this. Caroline, careful, you lucky girl.

Our stream is narrow, especially in the summer. Here is the pool we dug to get drinking water and down below there's another for washing on hot days. We have tubs and barrels that collect rainwater in other places. The latrine, a trench with a bag of lime hidden in the bushes, is further away and we dig a new one every two weeks. There are right ways to do everything in the forest park so you won't draw attention. If you sharpen a pencil you pick up the shavings. If you burn paper there's still ashes.

Back toward home I switch the full water bucket from one hand to the other, the empty chamber pot in the tired hand. I look all around as I get close. We have moved three times since we came to live in the forest park and I don't want to move again. There's not even anyone in the trees except the birds and they're singing now that the sky is getting brighter.

Father is sleeping, exactly the same. He twitches all of a sudden like maybe the start of a helicopter dream and then he settles. Sometimes right when he's falling asleep he'll jerk his arms and legs too and he might wake himself up or kick me a little.

Silent I set down the pot and bucket. The flat stones are still cold so I stand on one foot then the other. I could climb in bed and read but my feet might touch him and wake him so instead I turn and climb the tall tree where the lookout is.

Ferns grow up high in the trees too, in the branches though not so high as where I am in the lookout. Squirrels chitter and chatter, now circling up and down tree trunks after each other. It's an easy climb for me especially barefoot, the branches mostly like a ladder. The platform is almost one hundred feet high, Father says and the bottom, the boards are covered over with branches attached on so you cannot see it from the ground. On the platform I can see all around us. I can see the pale flat stones that don't look like a path unless you know it's a path, which we step on so we don't make a trail. I see the place where my hidden garden is hidden and the branch across the front of our house which you could never see since the roof can be walked on and ferns are growing there like the rest of the ground and even the tiny maples with their five-pointed leaves. Our house is like a cave dug out with the roof made of branches and wire and metal with tarps and plastic on top of that and then the earth where everything is growing. Only Father and I see it's a house.

I can see a long ways, between the trees. The forest park stretches eight miles across and our house is somewhere in the middle. It goes up a mile from our house to fields and farmhouses and then slants down steep for a mile the other way, to the road and the city, the railyard and all the metal pieces and trucks and storage containers that Father says people can live inside. The pale green of the St. Johns Bridge, stretching across the river to the Safeway and the library and everything on that side. A long ship in the river with a red line around it, close along the water.

A rustle beneath me now and the branch below shivers, tips out, Father's hand showing and then his voice sounding.

"Where's my girl?" he says.

"Up high," I say.

By the time I'm down the green Coleman stove is out on its flat stone and the kettle is on it, the stove's blue flame spitting and catching. You have to listen closely so the water doesn't boil away since Father took the whistler off the spout.

Breakfast is cold oatmeal and dried apricots and hot water to drink.

"Heading into the city today," he says.

"Tomorrow," I say. "It's Tuesday today."

"We're low on things," he says. "Milk powder, oatmeal. Your appetite keeps growing."

"I'm growing," I say.

"Exactly," he says and he's smiling, the lines all around his eyes. "Anyways," he says, "the thing about schedules and routines is they're good to have for you but you don't want everyone to be able to predict you, either."

We change into our city clothes. Our forest clothes are darker so no one can see us and they can get dirtier but if someone sees you like that in the city they think all sorts of things. I put on my tan blouse and brown pants and braid back my hair.

"Beware of all enterprises that require new clothes," Father says. He laughs and pulls his shirt over his head and I see my name, Caroline, tattooed on his arm up high on his shoulder in cursive letters and then he buttons on his pale yellow city shirt with the collar.

Father's red frame pack has the metal wrapped with black tape so it won't shine. My pack is blue and has no metal. In the men's camp they let their garbage pile up but we don't. We carry it out in our packs, inside plastic bags. I put Randy in too with his head sticking out through the zipper and we're ready to go.

"Sweetheart," Father says, a name I like.

He has a book in one hand, he always carries a book. For me the encyclopedias are too heavy and the dictionary is not good to read since it keeps you going back and forth without ever slowing down to tell you enough about a thing which is not a way I like to read.

It's pretty in the morning walking down our secret path under the trees and the sun. You can buy a map of all the trails of the forest park but our paths won't be on it. Our paths run along next to some of those paths and fire lanes and trails for city people but they are different. I am behind Father and his hair is getting longer now so he's pressed it down with water. It is black and dark gray.

"How come," I say, "when I cut your hair you say the birds take the hair and use it in their nests and you still make us go so far away from home when only the birds are going to see it and then move it around?"

"We just do," he says.

The leaves are like lace, the sun shining through. Red berries grow on the bushes. We climb over deadfalls, their roots up in the sky. Some trees fall into other trees and never hit the ground but rest like the hypotenuse of a triangle slanting in the air. In the wind they groan as they rub against the tree that holds them or in a storm they can come crashing down.

Father stops walking. "I have a feeling," he says. He sniffs the air.

"Why?" I say.

"Not a good feeling," he says. "Let's go back."

"We're almost to the bridge," I say. "We're almost out of milk powder. You said."

"Caroline," he says. "Listen to me."

"Yes," I say. "I know. I just thought."

"There are more important things to do today," he says. "Not in these clothes, though. We have to change."

WITH THE WIRE I carried from the salvage yard we build a hiding place, in case we have to hide if someone is after us. Most times it is better not to let people know we are here at all. We scoop out and dig down between trunks where many trees have fallen. Between the trunks, beneath where the dead sharp branches stretch out we dig hollows a little bigger than our bodies. We scoop and then we lay down to test the size and then we scoop out some more. Once they're big enough Father takes the wire and plastic bags and piles dirt and leaves and sticks on top like a trapdoor that looks like the ground and covers the holes. Hiding holes. I practice lifting up the cover and sliding in and Father checks to see how it looks and then he practices and I check and where he is it looks just like the ground.

"How about that?" he says. "Now we just have to remember where they are, since they're so hard to see."

Father can whistle in ways that fools birds. One finger, two fingers, no fingers. Breathing in or blowing out. Loud or soft.

"I could make a snare," he says. "I could catch a squirrel or rabbit, if we ate meat."

"Could you catch them without hurting them?" I say.

"Probably," he says. "Maybe."

"Why don't you?" I say. "Not for pets, but just to look at them up close. For homework."

There's crying in the air and we stop and watch a bunch of black crows chasing an eagle around in the sky until they slide too far out to the left and we can't see them anymore. We start walking again.

"I could easily do that," Father says, "if I wanted to. I could even make a snare that would catch a person."

"A person?" I say.

"He'd have no idea," Father says. "Until it was too late. Jerk him straight upside down, swinging by his heels."

I AM A PERSON who likes to be alone since I am never alone, exactly. It is important that we have time in solitude, Father says, and before he wanted to keep me in sight when he was working on something or at least make an agreement on how far I could go but now that I'm older I am allowed to range, except not leave the forest park's boundaries, and I am to stay off the roads and main trails. I have to hear or see anyone before they can see or hear me, and hide out of the way. We call this alone time, when we go out by ourselves.

I like to go barefoot. It is almost impossible to climb a tree wearing shoes. I cannot go barefoot in the city since it is dangerous and does not look right so it draws attention. In the woods it is fine. It is also fine to sing in the woods but there is no reason to sing loudly. If you can hear yourself, that is enough. If you had a friend you could walk close together and sing softly. With my fingernail I scratch words into some of the leaves around. Hello friend, I scratch, and the green goes darker under my fingernail so someone walking along might read that. It's not good to leave any signs but still I do this. I do not collect things since collections draw attention. It is possible to collect things in your mind or to gather them and one way to do this is to write them. I will never scratch anything into the bark of a tree since that hurts them but sometimes I will onto a leaf.

The alone time is strict on our watches. Father and I wear matching watches. We set them to match each other. The time on our two watches only matches each other since that's how we set them. If everyone else's time says it's four o'clock our watches might say eleven-fifteen. If the clock on the bank says nine forty-five, our watches might say six-thirty. We change them every few days. If I ever take my watch off I buckle it around Randy's middle, like a saddle next to my blue ribbon, and that way I'll never forget it. I keep it on when I'm sleeping and if my hand is under the pillow I can still hear it ticking.

Father used to say I had to be back at dusk but he learned it's safer for me at night since I know what I'm doing and there's almost no one around. My eyes adjust. It's easy. The animals don't even expect me. I startle possum, raccoons out across the clearings into deeper shadows or across the shiny streets below. I hardly have my hands out in front of me. I can smell when an animal is close.

Quiet I slip to the edge of the trees where broken fences lean. Lights shine through the windows so stretched yellow squares rest in backyards. At a house I can see dogs inside with just their thick heads and pointed ears and curved tails up in the windows. I stop and watch. I try to whistle high like Father can but they just keep walking around without any notice and their tails wagging.

A boy comes out the back door holding something black in his hands. He has square eyeglasses in dark frames around his eyes. The moon stretches his shadow at me and he walks to the edge of his yard and stares where the trees come down thick. He walks from one end to the other.

"What are you looking for?" I say. My voice is not loud, not a whisper.

He is already halfway to the house, hardly looking back.

"Wait," I say. "Don't be afraid. Come back." I step out a little, just so he can see my face.

He squints at me, says nothing. Then he steps a little closer, fifteen feet, a kind of fence between us.

"Are you a real girl?" he says.

"What did you think I was, a ghost?"

"I don't know."

"I'm real," I say. "What's your name?"

"Zachary."

"Do you go to a real school?" I say.

"It's summer vacation," he says. "Are you wearing shoes?"

"No," I say. "I can't tell what's in your hand."

"My camera," he says. "Can I take your picture?"

"No," I say. "Are those your dogs in there?"

"Yes."

"You can let them out. I like dogs. I'm not afraid. Do they have fleas?"

He's closer. He's not so afraid of me now but if I leaped forward he'd probably still run. He's smaller than me and I came out of the dark forest.

"You thought I was a ghost," I say.

"You're a girl," he says. "Where do you live?"

"In a house with my father."

"What school do you go to?"

"At home," I say. "What are you looking for, out here?"

"A man," he says. "A kind of man, maybe. Maybe not a man."

"What?"

"He lives in the woods and the dogs are afraid of him. He's quick and quiet. He never talks at all. I don't even know if he can."

"Maybe not a man?" I say.

The boy looks up at the moon and the stars. "I think," he says, "I think he might be a Bigfoot."

I laugh.

"Don't," he says. "I told you. You don't know."

"I laughed since I know," I say. "I know what you're talking about. I know him. That's the way he is."

"Where is he?"

"Around," I say. "He could be listening right now, but I doubt it. His name is Nameless, which is kind of a joke. He used to have a name. I've talked to him before."

"You couldn't talk to him," he says. "Is that a horse in your hand?"

"Yes," I say. "His name is Randy."

"The man or the horse?"

"The horse," I say. "He's a special horse."

A woman's voice calls out from the house: "Zachary? Who are you talking to out there? What are you doing?"

The boy turns to look and when he turns back I am already in the shadows gone, silent as I slip between the trees still thinking of him. Zachary. How long did we talk? Five minutes? He was only a boy, maybe ten, so much younger than me but sometimes it is all right or easier to be friends with a boy who is not your age. We had talked like we were friends, about his camera and Nameless and about Randy.

"Thanks, Randy," I say, whispering into the hole in his stomach. "Zachary," I say.

The round hole in Randy's stomach is not wide. It can be covered by my fingertip, which is how I hold him even though almost nothing would get inside him and nothing would fall out. Two things I have put in there: a small shiny stone that I found in the stream and a scrap of paper rolled up tight where I have written a secret secret in case I ever forget it. You would have to cut Randy open to get anything out of him.

You could cut him on the seam between white side and his painted side that shows his muscles and organs like his skin is torn off. Heart, liver, kidney, lungs. Horses' bodies are not the same as humans' but still I can learn from the painted side as I have the same organs inside my body. So do you. The white side has red dots with black numbers by them, where I practice my arithmetic. Add this and this, Father says, pointing on Randy's body, now take this away from that, now multiply these. There are one hundred and fourteen numbers and the ones closest to Randy's mouth are 19 and 20 like he is saying them. The numbers around his eye are 7, 8, 9, 10, 12. The number 11 is right on his eyeball so anything he'd see on that side has a dot and that number like looking through a glass window with writing on it. Only that makes things backward but 11 is the same both ways. Father gave Randy to me and when I first got him he smelled like a chemical and paint. Now he smells like nothing at all so maybe he smells like me. I touch my tongue to him and he tastes like salt from my hands.

I've made it all the way back deep into the forest park without even paying attention since my bare feet know the way so well and my mind has been thinking about other things. Animals might have passed close by me and thought I was sleepwalking.

Listening for my own breath which I cannot hear I hear shouting instead. Men's voices from the camp. I spin and ease closer with now the sun down and not any shadows so it's easy to get close. Around the fire I don't see Nameless or even Richard, just a bunch of men eating and drinking things and smoking cigarettes with their dogs sleeping by the fire whose ears raise up and then droop down since the smoke is in their noses and they can't tell where or who or even if I'm out here.

———

THE POST OFFICE is just over the St. Johns Bridge, on Ivanhoe Street. I rush to our box and lean my eye to the little window and there is one envelope inside. It's Father's check that the government sends him every month for being in a war. He opens the envelope, looks at the check, then puts it back in the envelope and folds it and puts it in his front pocket.

Outside again we pass the flea market where Father bought his frame pack, then Burgerville and Dad's Restaurant which Father won't take me to even as a joke. A pointed blue sign says WELCOME TO HISTORIC ST. JOHNS ESTABLISHED IN 1847. St. Johns is a neighborhood, not a city. It's in the city of Portland, in the state of Oregon, in the country of the United States of America. It's summer. The year is 1999. Up Lombard at the theater the sign says BLAIR WITCH PROJECT.

"Is that about witches?" I say.

"We'll never know," Father says. He's whistling. He has his elbows bent and his hands hooked inside the black straps of his pack.

As we go we put some of our garbage in a trash can when no one is looking and put some in another as we walk further down the street. It is a lot happening at once when we go to the city. Signs blink. A bus leans when turning a corner. I hurry past a black dog tied to a parking meter. We pass a homeless man with a shopping cart full of things. I push the crosswalk button and the man in the sign blinks and we cross the street. Two girls younger than me coast by on bicycles. One is pink, the other yellow. I do not know how to ride a bicycle since we have no place to keep one and since Father says I'd get too far away. He is the tallest person in the city. He looks in the window at the Salvation Army where we sometimes get our clothes and we keep on, past Urban Soul Tattoo.

"Are there really witches?" I say.

"I've never met one," Father says.

We don't go into the Tulip Bakery. Sometimes there are children in the playground across the street but not today since we're earlier than usual or it's a different day. Already I can see the red brick library with its white pillars. We cross again, close to the school, then go up the steps.

Inside there's a shiny desk. The children's books are to the right and all the tables and chairs on that side are smaller.

"Hello," says the librarian. "My best customers."

"So much to read," Father says.

"Hello," I say. "It's me, Caroline."

"Enough," Father says, since I'm not supposed to tell strangers my name. He leads me deeper into all the books.

Once I've gotten through the encyclopedias all these books will be easy and make sense for me. All the books of the library, filling all the shelves and shelves. The hinges of books are called spines and are all different colors. I see the spines of the encyclopedias, all the letters I don't have but that we'll get when I need them. My library card is in the front pocket of my city pants. Usually I don't check anything out. Father usually renews books he already has.

The librarian is typing with her back toward us, her dark hair is braided like my hair is braided and her cardigan sweater is bright blue. She is a quiet lady. She smiles when she sees us, so she is no stranger. She loves everyone who reads books. Every time she looks at me I can feel it and it's not like sometimes with some people. With her she's thinking the best thoughts and liking me. While I am looking at the spines of all the books she passes close behind me and touches my back up high with the flat of her hand. She has probably read every book in the library.

"Caroline," Father says. "Let's go."

"Goodbye," the librarian says. "See you soon, I hope."

At the Safeway, Father takes the check out of his pocket and writes on the back of it and then puts it in another envelope and feeds it into the wall of the ATM. Next the money comes out and he folds it and puts it in his pocket.

The lights hum, inside Safeway, up by the voices that call out of speakers. They are an unhealthy kind of light to be under and so we hurry. Father's in the bathroom by the bakery department, shaving, and I'm buying what we need by the time he's done.

Outside, the sun has shifted around so it can be in our faces both ways, coming and going. On the way home it's pulling me back. A car passes us and I pretend I'm inside it and I close my eyes and take ten steps. I can hardly see how far the car has gone, slipping away. I'd be all the way ahead, but slow is not always bad. Father says a car is an anchor. He says machines cause as many problems as they solve.

The St. Johns Bridge has two tall green towers with two black points on top of each one with red lights at the very tips. For planes to see or maybe for lightning. It's always windy here, even on still days. Only some of the bridge is over the river and down below the remains of old piers stick like whiskers through the dark water. Father shaves in the summer and grows a beard in the winter. Bright red cuts on his neck from the razor, he walks on the side facing the traffic and I am along the rail, looking down at the rusty railroad bridge that can lift for boats and further to all the other bridges of the city to my left. The tall buildings look so small from here, five miles away.

We squint into the sun. A dog barks, so close to my ears, in the back of a truck speeding past. I look back behind us where airplanes slide in and rise up from the airport. I've never been on an airplane, not that I can remember. Further than the airport there are mountains. Mount Hood in snow a little to the right, and Mount St. Helens, a volcano on the left. They are too far to walk to. If we had a car we could drive to them but we will never have a car.

The bridge shakes and trembles beneath my feet. Halfway across is almost halfway home. The trees are a solid changing green and as you come closer they break apart and separate so you can see how it works. Looking up to the left I can see all the green trees of the forest park and can guess where our home is, where someone in the lookout could see us now. Someone could walk into our house if they could find it and we couldn't do anything about it. At least Randy is with me, and Father, who could make another house any time or place.

We're almost to the forest park when I see the orange spots against the green trees.

"What are those orange men doing?" I say.

"Who?" Father squints. "Criminals," he says.

"What are they doing?"

"Whatever those police say. You see those two men? And that white truck has dogs in it, so if any of the criminals tries to run away they let the dogs loose to catch them."

"How many dogs?" I squint to see the truck better but it is far away.

"Those men have to clean up all along the highway," Father says, "and cut back the tall grass since they did something wrong and got caught."

"They did a crime," I say. "Criminals."

"Exactly," Father says.

"Like what?"

"Let's walk. Don't worry about them, Caroline. We have ourselves to worry about, and that's plenty."

The red spots on his neck have dried and I reach up and brush them off.

"Thank you, Caroline," he says.

"Shaver," I say.

FATHER IS STRICT. He has to be strict. That doesn't mean he knows everything I do or think. There are all kinds of things he's taught me and ways I've taught myself and things I've learned. There's the animals and then there's sounds and actions and feelings that not even the trees or plants are making. I am the one who knows about food in the forest park, the best places for blackberries and when the morels are up I know where to find them and the mushroom harvests are maybe when we eat best. There are ferns you can also eat and of course the things I grow. Once I found a patch of mint growing wild by just the smell and also wild ginger but those are more flavors than food.

Sometimes a stone will roll up a hill. Or a stone will leap in the air and rap against another stone or a tree like he is angry at them. I have seen this happen. I have seen a fallen tree slowly right itself and its dead branches will sprout leaves.

One alone time I hear a noise and see Father behind a bush, watching me which is not what he is supposed to be doing. I can use his tricks against him, though. I can be more patient than him, wait for his attention to drift. I do things he doesn't know about and I have places where he's never been.

I have my own lookout all covered in branches, high off the ground. I climb into it and rest on my back. The sound of the wind is wonderful and always changing. The airplanes fly over with their sound. They leap from space to space between the trees. I hear the dogs coming and turn over on my stomach.

They bite at each others' shoulders and get snarled up and plow sideways into the bushes but let loose so they don't fall behind and can catch up. I think the head dog is a girl dog, brown and without a collar even if some of the dogs have collars and Lala just keeps running and running and the other dogs, some of them might be coyotes but Father says that's impossible even if there are coyotes in the forest park. The other dogs are all shapes and sizes and all different colors. There are usually more than ten but not twenty and today almost twenty. They follow Lala since they think she knows something or is going somewhere just by the way she runs and the truth is I think is that it's just that she likes to run so much and she's happy. I know how she feels.

Even after they are gone the bushes are still snapping back. I can still hear the sound of snarling and panting and breaking sticks.

Now Father comes walking silently through the trees, a brown paper bag in his hand. Even from up high he looks tall. He wears his city clothes. His hair is shiny, wet down and his face is smooth. I duck down before he looks behind him or checks the sky like he does. I am down on the ground behind him and he doesn't hear. I follow.

He looks all around again before he steps out of the forest and onto the street, the sidewalk. His steps are long. I am after him. Still barefoot I'm careful, one block almost away and I'm shivering even though the sun is not quite down and it's warm. I can feel people in the houses looking out and the people in the cars driving by and I don't know what Father would say if I catch up or if he looks back. I'm afraid. My breath is hard. I turn and race back to the forest park, the safe dark shadows of the trees stretching out to meet me. Back inside I breathe slow, easier. I am walking deeper and I am thinking it's fine if Father has secrets since I have secrets. We trust. And I am also thinking that it is not okay to have a secret where he leaves me behind even if I'm being alone.

I can now run for five minutes without slowing at all. I practice. With only Randy in my hand I leap over stumps, ferns, check my watch, circle back, practice being able to breathe after all that without making a sound.

THE HINGED BACK of a book. Strength of character or strength of willpower. A sharp or bony projection such as found on a porcupine.

———

THE SUNLIGHT is still not down to us and the ground is damp and cool. Father's red frame pack is full and the only thing in my pack is Randy.

"Wear shoes," Father says.

"Why?"

"They don't have to know everything about the way we are," he says. "Let's go."

We do not walk in a straight line to the men's camp. We take a different path every time so we don't wear down a trail and lead people to us.

As we walk he says the kind of thing he always says: "You notice how there are no women there at night, no girls who sleep there, how you've never seen a baby there. That's because it's too dangerous, because the men can't be trusted. You notice how they move their camp all the time and how only the rangers pick up after them. They break into the hikers' cars in the parking lot and steal things and that draws plenty of attention, you know. Without the men's camp, our lives would be easier, here."

"Still," I say, "we barter with them. How come I get no summer vacation from school?"

He doesn't answer. He just grunts and leads the way. Mapleseed pods spin down, helicoptering, but I don't use that word.

I hear Father's name and mine shouted from above, a lookout in the trees. If we wanted to slip in without them seeing we could but today it doesn't matter.

The flies are on my face and hands already. Father is slapping them away from his own face. There are always flies everywhere here since the men don't hardly dig latrines or they don't go far enough and let trash pile up too. When the flies get too bad or if the rangers break it up they just move the camp and you some- times walk through where an old camp has been and there's still trash and fire rings and everything is beaten down and foul and it takes a long time for anything to grow.

The friendly dogs reach us first, jumping up to lick, their dirty paws.

"Fleas," Father warns me. "Remember what happened last time."

The long grass is all stomped down and there are cigarette butts all around and shreds of plastic bags. Clarence with the red beard is older and mostly in charge. He sees us and stands and walks across. He's already licking his lips around inside that beard and reaching out his scabby hands to hold the things that Father is unpacking.

Behind Clarence is Richard, who is looking at me. He has drawn lightning bolts in black pen on the sides of his jeans and he's wearing a bright orange T-shirt that anyone could see through the forest from a mile away. He's twenty or so, Richard. His bleached out hair is pulled into rubber bands like ten nubby horns on top of his head. He won't get too close or talk straight to me since he's afraid of Father.

"I'll show you something," he says like he's not talking to me, and then he walks on his hands with his boots kicking the air so mud flies off. He does a cartwheel and a round off and leaps sideways making sure I'm watching.

I stay close like Father said but I don't watch or listen to the bartering. There are too many people around, not to mention Richard who is looking sideways at me and rocking from foot to foot like he might try another trick while he is singing this song I've heard him sing before, all about the girl with my name who lost her long hair and who used to be happy and who cannot be found:

"Oh, Caroline, no," he sings. "Who took that look away?"

"Could you shut up?" Father says and Richard turns away, quiet, and all the dogs' ears prick at the sound of Father's deep voice. These are not the ones that run with Lala, these always stay near the men and sometimes have ropes around their necks and will sometimes be in the city when the men are begging on a sidewalk since people will give money if they see a dog.

There are three different fires going and that's one place you can really get warm even though I understand why Father does not allow fires. One man at the nearest one has his feet almost in the fire and he's fallen backward over a log and is stretched out snoring with his back in the mud.

The shredded paper people are skinnier than the Skeletons and they're twitchy, crouched around as they fit pages and words together, trying to find out something they can use to get money or something. Names and numbers, Father told me. Credit cards and social security numbers. They don't look up for anyone or any sound. They hardly have any teeth.

Over at the furthest away fire is a group of people I know. They are a family of people but they are not actually a family they just all stay together like one since it's safer. I call them the Skeleton Family in my mind since they're so skinny. The oldest ones are named Johnny and Isabel who are like the parents even if they aren't the parents. They tell everyone what to do. They don't sleep at the men's camp I think but sometimes visit.

A girl named Valerie waves at me and I wave back and the way she waves is like we're still friends and she knows that I can't go over there by her Skeleton Family and have to stay close to Father. He will shout if I go closer.

A few times here I played with Valerie. The Skeletons mostly live in the city which is one reason Father doesn't like them. They beg money and maybe steal. They only sleep in the forest park if they're afraid or if the police are sweeping or something so Father says if they're here it's bad for everyone. People were never supposed to live in cities. They gathered together since they were scared and then living like that only made them more and more afraid. Valerie is nice, though. She is a year older than me and hasn't hardly read any books at all and says she doesn't care. Last time she had a kitten that she let me pet. Black and white with runny eyes it could barely walk.

"Okay, Caroline," Father says. "Let's go now."

In two minutes the flies let up and the air is sweet again. It's like there are more birds and the leaves of the trees are greener the further away we walk.

"Richard," Father says, "stopped getting smarter a long time ago. You're finished speaking with him."

"Yes," I say. "It's weird," I say. "Going there."

"If you're going to say something," Father says, "be specific. You just said nothing at all."

"Well," I say, "you can go there and do nothing, really, and still when you leave you just feel tired."

"That's because of the way they live," he says. "They're tired all the time and they don't even know it. You're right,

Caroline. However good the bartering, it's just not worth it. And today? Just these two blue tarps, one ripped. Not much, but better than having to carry all that junk we traded all the way back down to the city. Still, you're right. That's the last time we go there."

"Ever?" I say.

"I don't know if we're getting better," he says, "or they're getting worse or both, but it's just gotten to this point. And it's not good for either one of us, being exposed to that. Now look here," he says, and pulls back the bushes.

We're back at the dead deer and there are only a few tufts of hair, a dried-out strip of skin. The white skull is stripped clean and part of the rib cage and the bones are scattered around disappearing into the bushes like the skeleton fell out of the sky and shattered in every direction.

"Look at this, Caroline," Father says. "If you were in a schoolhouse you could never learn like this. You're going to be the smartest of them all."

We look at the deer a while longer, kicking gently with the toes of our shoes, before we turn and start back for home, walking again.

"You really don't like Richard," I say.

"What's to like?" Father says. "He's a fool."

"What about Nameless?"

"He wasn't there, was he? He's gone."

"He's still in the forest park," I say. "Just not in the camp. He left it."

"A fool also," Father says. "Have you seen him?"

"Where else would he go?" I say.

"We have the liveliest interest in a wild man," Father says. "They feel the impulse from the vernal wood."

Father will talk like this sometimes, saying things like he memorized them and someone said them before or he read them in a book. It's a hard thing to answer.

"But Nameless left the camp so maybe he's smart," I say. "He doesn't steal and he eats what he finds. He can run faster on all fours than most people can run on two legs."

"The liveliest interest!" Father says, his voice rising.

"What?" I say. "Do you think a person can really eat banana slugs? Richard told me that Nameless does."

"Maybe," Father says. "Look that up in your books, or next time we're at the library. Why not? People eat snails."

"Snails?" I say.

"What are you so worked up about?" Father says. He reaches his hand out and pulls me close, the side of my body against the side of his body. "You don't need to worry about these people," he says. "You're better than they are. Smarter and more civilized. We've already worked so hard. Are you ready to study this afternoon? Geometry?"

"Chess first?" I say.

"Only one game," he says, but once we get home and get settled we play three and the last one takes longer than half an hour.

In chess the knight is a horse and he moves in the shape of an L. I wonder what Randy thinks about that as a way to get around.

TWO SQUIRRELS are chasing each other like they're not really fighting but playing like they're friends. Squirrels' memories are much shorter than ours even if their lives are much shorter too so maybe they remember more carefully and that's what sets them twitching and jerking around. In alone time I like to follow but it's not always easy to follow a squirrel. It depends what it's up to or where it wants to go and when two are chasing each other that makes it trickier so I just keep walking.

To follow a bird is impossible. I can follow a banana slug or some ants for hours and that whole time my thoughts slip away and I have to keep bringing myself back to remind me what the insects are doing.

People are easy to follow, and it's amazing the things they do when they think no one can see them. I follow joggers or even Richard or men I don't know from the men's camp and no one ever knows I'm there.

This morning a boy and girl come walking up the gravel road in the middle of the forest park called Leif Ericksen Drive. At first I think they are two boys. In the trees alongside the road, fifteen feet away, I walk like they are, keeping up. The girl holds a piece of yellow candy in her teeth and the boy snatches it, puts it in his mouth and I wonder if I were there, their third friend, if he would pass the candy to me so I could try it since I am not allowed to eat candy. They are my age or barely older.

The boy and girl slip down a side trail and I stay higher on my own trail. They're down in a hollow where there's a clearing and a tall round blue water tank with a flat top and a ladder I can't reach. That's where they climb and start to dance around with their arms like they are pretending to swim. Then the girl takes off her shirt and the boy is in his white underwear and sits down. The girl keeps dancing so her dark hair comes loose and her white shirt leaps all the way down and is caught in some bushes below, her shoes kicked off and her bra but I can't see much. I can hear myself breathing as I watch. She sits down next to him, close like they are talking and then after a while she puts her bra back on and stands and goes back to the ladder and slides down a rope the last ten feet. She finds her shirt and her back-pack where she left it. The boy comes down after and then I lose track even if I could still follow if I wanted.

Father and I are supposed to meet at home at eleven to go over my homework but I'm over an hour early so I take the E encyclopedia and climb into the lookout. It's impossible to climb with both the encyclopedia and Randy so I take two trips. No horse has ever been higher in trees. Then I lie on the narrow platform on my back, the book beneath my head and Randy on my chest and I think a while.

An airplane slides along, the white line behind it. Far away I can hear cars on the freeway, a sound I wouldn't recognize if Father hadn't told me.

It is already a hot day, the legs of my pants rolled up almost to my knees and I am thinking of standing and taking off my clothes and hanging them in the branches around since some-times in my alone time I like to look carefully at my body to see how it's been changing. There is a way that bodies can look that mine is starting to look like. The white bra of the girl on the water tank, the shape of her makes me think, makes me want to check my own body.

I have my shirt pulled off down to my undershirt when I hear cracking sticks below, branches pulled back and whipping around and then coming closer I hear breathing. Huffing and puffing is the only way to say it. I turn over onto my stomach and peek over just as a man comes busting into the clearing.

He is running. He is a runner. He has on white shoes and red shorts and a gray tank top and a white band like a halo around his long brown hair that is bald on top. Around his waist he has a belt that has little plastic canteens on it. He looks like he's run a long way and when he hits our clearing he stops and puts his hands on his knees and spits on the ground. Looking down he sees something through the branch across our door and steps closer and tips it away. He bends down and looks in and steps back and spits again, right next to the door of our house.

I make a little noise in my throat when he spits like that. I don't mean to and somehow then he looks up and sees me. His face is shiny from sweating and he turns all the way around shielding his eyes and I slide back so he cannot see me. I try to see him through the slats in the platform, through the branches attached on underneath and I cannot. I hold my breath. Randy is half under me sharp in my ribs.

"Hello?" the man says. "Hi? Girl? Don't be afraid."

I'm afraid he might try to climb the tree and I turn a little so I can kick down on his hands if he tries it. I breathe silently and hold my breath again. I can hear the man breathing, below, his steps on the grass we try not to ever step on. Minutes pass. I can hear my watch tick, and after a long time I hear a branch snap down low and heavy steps and more silence.

When I look over he is gone and no one is below and I see how my shirt is still off, hanging on the branch above me and that's what the man's eye caught on and how he saw me at all which was a stupid mistake.

A breeze kicks up and shivering I put my shirt back on over my undershirt. The green leaves still slide thick above, the sky pale blue past that. Branches rub against each other, back and forth, a slow creak. Squirrels and birds rattle from tree to tree. The air up here does not smell like dirt. It's sharper, closer to the sun. People have seen me in the forest park before but never so close to our house. That is a rule that has not been broken before and I do not want to make another house. I stretch out, my head on the encyclopedia and my hand around Randy, my fingertips on the edges of his organs. I watch the green leaves above. I try to concentrate, to look for airplanes.

"Caroline?" Father says, all of a sudden below. "My heart?"

"Here," I say. "Up high."

"You're all right? What in hell happened here?"

I look over to see the branch tipped over, the grass tromped down by the runner.

"I don't know," I say. "Everything was this way when I came back so I climbed up here to be safe."

"Good girl," he says. "You come down, now."

Later while he's reading Father looks up and says, "Are you sure you didn't see anything today? It seems like we'll have to move again."

"No," I say.

"You didn't see anything?"

"Not here," I say. "By the water tank I saw a boy and a girl."

"That's what you're writing about?"

"Yes."

"And what were they doing?"

"Taking off their clothes."

"Taking off their clothes?" he says. "Why would they do that? To get a suntan?"

"I don't think so," I say. "I don't know. Maybe to see what their bodies looked like."

IT'S LATE IN THE afternoon on a Friday and I hear the sound of dogs barking and echoing like they're in a cave or something. Usually when I hear them their barks are getting louder so they're running closer to me or they're fading away so the dogs are running in another direction. This time the loudness and so the distance isn't changing and I try another direction, walking, where it gets louder as I go and I hurry on down the slope.

I squint my ears and still can't tell if it's Lala. What it is is all the barking comes out of one white metal truck and even a hundred feet away through tall grass waving in the wind I can see the word CANINE painted on the side. I can see dark shapes and shadows back behind the bars. It's a truck full of dogs.

And the tall grass between the truck and me isn't really waving in the wind, it's chopping back and forth with pieces tossed in the air. Flashes of orange break through, and arms with long tools. It's the men again in their orange outfits, the criminals cutting down the tall grass. Still walking closer, I slow and stay in the shadows. I notice two men between the criminals and the truck, now, holding rifles pointed in the air. If a criminal tried to run away into the forest park they might shoot him or they might let the dogs loose to chase him. I sit and think that the dogs might not care once they were up in the trees where I am. They might just keep running until they meet up with my dogs and could run along with them all night. This is what I'm thinking when I look up and a man is closer, chopping at the grass. He stops to rest, wiping his black face with an orange sleeve. He sees me and he stares.

I step further back into the shadow and then turn and begin to run slipping back and forth through the trees up the slope. Behind me I can hear nothing but the dogs' echoing barking and then even that fades away so I know they're not after me.

I don't reach out for the blackberries along the trail since Friday is the day we fast which makes me hungry and I don't feel strong but you get used to it by the afternoon. The thorns on the vines scratch me as I go.

I slow and check around and I'm close to my secret lookout so I circle and come in the other way and climb up and stretch out, resting. The sky is hazy and hot, not exactly clouds.

I close my eyes and all at once there's a cracking like the dogs but no barking anywhere. I peek over and Nameless is coming. On all fours he shoots down a pathway then darts on his feet sideways over a stone and ducks low beneath a sword fern. He steps out, checking his trail to see the marks he made, if he made any. Then he backs up and does it all over again. I can tell that he's practicing.

"Hey," I say, hissing down at him. "Nameless."

He doesn't look up until I break a stick from a dead branch and throw it down at him. His face is blacked out and his teeth and eyes are both more yellow than I remember.

"You're smart to get out of the men's camp," I say. "We're never going back there again. You could say my name," I say. "Or don't. Just look at me." But he doesn't except out of the side of his eye.

He turns away and I start to climb down before he's gone.

"There's criminals over there," I say. "And dogs."

Halfway down the tree I can see him starting to go through his routine again like he can't even tell I'm there. I wait until he comes back into the clearing.

"You're not deaf," I say. I jump down and step right in front of him so he has to look at me and when he does it's like he's going to smile and then he doesn't make any expression at all. Up close it isn't dirt on his face but blackberry juice, smashed on and sticky. That's what's clumping his hair together too. A fly lands under his eye and he doesn't brush it away. I do and he leaps back like I pinched him.

"Nameless," I say. "Haven't I always been your friend?"

His breath is foul like dirt and like he really does eat bugs and banana slugs. He breathes through his mouth which is a loud way to breathe. Around his ankles are what look like rawhide shoelaces.

"Those could trip you," I say, pointing, and he doesn't even look down. I say, "If they snagged on something or something. What, you think it's pretty funny to see if I get frustrated? Listen, I don't have to talk to you."

My voice is louder than I want it to sound and still I keep talking fast like that will hold him there and finally make him answer.

"I met a boy who thinks you're a Bigfoot," I say, and for a moment I think he's actually listening and might say something. "Does that make you happy?" I say. "You know, just because you're so dirty doesn't mean anything. My name is Caroline, in case you forgot it."

Now he really turns away and I don't care but I follow him anyway, just to show that I can. It's dusk now but my eyes are adjusted. Nameless is really going on all fours, not crawling exactly since his feet are on the ground so his butt is up in the air and he's practicing spinning around behind trees to hide and when he stop he sniffs at the air like he can smell something but really if he could he'd know that I'm following him which he doesn't know. So I stop following and let him go since I don't know what else I would say.

So I walk all the way down by Balch Creek where it's cool even on the hottest days. I go on a side path past the broken down stone house and I backtrack where I cross a trail that's on a map and I walk backward for a while, putting my heels down first so anyone would think that I'd gone where I'd come from when actually I am in another place entirely. I am walking in the dusk through the last stand of trees, toward the first houses and I can see their black rooftops through the leaves closer to me and also lights in some of the windows.

But there are no lights in Zachary's windows and I watch a long time almost twenty minutes and do not see any dogs inside or anyone. After another ten minutes it's dark out and I climb the short wire fence and step across the yard. I knock on the back door and the sound is small so I knock again louder. I decide that if Zachary comes out and talks to me I'll let him take my picture this time.

Headlights flash along the side of the house and a car's engine chokes down. I run back to the fence, climb it, drop down low. No one comes. I wait another ten minutes and nothing changes at Zachary's house. All the windows are dark and quiet.

I check my watch again but there's two hours left of alone time and all I want is to see Father since I know at least he's a person who will actually talk with me. Nameless I am thinking about. How he tries to convince me he can't speak or tries to convince himself that he's changed like that or that a person can change like that. Once a person knows how to talk they know how unless they have a sore throat but that can't last forever and even then you can whisper. I'm thinking that Father and I will set up a snare and catch Nameless up just to show him who knows the forest park best and is not just pretending.

WE'VE ALMOST done my history homework and we're playing a game of chess when Father hears something I don't hear.

"Caroline," he says. Before he was talking softly, laughing, but his voice is a sharp whisper. "Quiet," he says. "Quick to the hiding holes."

A dog barks, a dog whines, closer to us. The chess pieces spill across the bed and we're running away, Father looking back and I'm keeping up afraid because of the look on his face and still thinking maybe it's a game or practice but the branches are snapping back behind him just over my head. We're not halfway to the hiding holes and there's a closer bark and the rasped breathing of a dog and a man shouts somewhere behind us. Above the birds escape through the branches of the trees.

Father reaches back for me. "Caroline," he says. "The trees."

I'm faster climbing and branches break off under his feet since he's so big but we're in the trees next to each other and twenty feet off the ground when the dogs arrive, really barking now. They don't pass us by, they sniff right to the bottom of the trees

and look up and there's no making friends with them. They leap
with their front paws clawing the bark and land and do it again.
They wear red vests that say POLICE in white letters. One is a
shepherd dog and the other has floppier ears and a looser face.
They keep on barking until the men arrive.

"Weapon!" one man shouts. "What's that in your hand, sir?
Drop it!"

"Bracelets," another man says. "Calm down."

There are six men and four are holding guns and two are
dressed in camouflage clothing like hunters. Two are policemen
and one is in tan-colored pants and a white shirt, sweating. The
last man is in regular clothes too. It takes a moment for me to see
that it's the runner who ran through our camp.

"Please," one policeman says. "Come slowly down from the
tree."

Father gets down first and they're all around him.

"There's no problem," he says.

"Then why were you running?"

"We didn't know who you were," he says. "And then we
were running since you were chasing us, and with the dogs."

"Slow, slow," a policeman says. "Do you have any identifi-
cation?"

"Not on me," Father says. "I'm a veteran, though. This is a
misunderstanding."

"I hope so," the policeman says.

I'm still in the tree, ten feet up. The other policeman has the
dogs back on their leashes and is feeding them something from a
pouch on his belt.

The men are very nervous with their guns out. They stay all around Father but when he moves in a direction they back up.

"It's a misunderstanding," he says again.

"Sir, stay where you are. Stop moving around."

He's trying to get closer to the tree where I am and I am trying to look back like he shouldn't worry.

"We need you to come along with us," the policeman says to Father. "Back to your camp, first. If you cooperate everything will be easier."

"Certainly," Father says. "There's no cause for handcuffs. I'd rather you didn't do this in front of my daughter."

The man with the tan pants and white shirt is beneath me now, wiping his head with a handkerchief, eyeglasses round around his eyes. He's reaching up like I need his help to get down.

"My name's James Harris," he says. "You can call me Jim. You'll come with me now."

"Father," I say.

"Trust me," Mr. Harris says. "We'll figure it all out."

Father's hands are behind his back and the men lead him away, back the way we'd come. After a moment Mr. Harris puts his hand on my shoulder. He's stayed behind with one police officer who stands in back of me when we start to walk after Father and the other men whose heads are lower than Father's and they're spread on all sides of him, walking with nervousness even though his arms are tied back.

"And what is your name?" Mr. Harris says. "Usually one person introduces themselves and then the other says their name."

"You can call me Caroline," I say.

"Is that your name?" he says.

"Yes," I say. "I said so."

"Caroline," he says, "this is Officer Stannard."

The policeman is walking behind me in case I try to run away and I almost laugh since I know that I could, that he couldn't catch me unless he let the dogs loose again and even then if I didn't climb a tree maybe I could gentle them. I almost want to try it but then that wouldn't help Father. I'm looking down at Mr. Harris's shiny black shoes with their pointed toes and slippery soles.

"Without the dogs you wouldn't have caught us," I say.

"We're trying to help you," he says.

"But you needed the dogs."

"That's probably true," he says, like that's not the point.

The dogs are up by Father, still wearing their red vests. I don't know if they would have smelled us if we'd reached the hiding holes in time. Mr. Harris stays close next to me and either can't walk any faster or is trying to slow us down. Soon I can't see Father ahead of us but I can hear the men's voices.

"This is a misunderstanding," I say but neither Mr. Harris or the policeman says anything. I wonder where Lala and my dogs are, or anyone who might help us.

When we get back to our house one of the camouflage men is gone and I don't see the dogs anywhere. Now I really could run, easily, but Father is facing away with his hands tied and when he tries to look around they try to turn him back. The runner is gone too, and two of the men are looking inside our house, then up at Father.

"I have some library books," he says. "Some other things I'd like to take, if we're going. My pack is the red one, there on the side. Yes. Come on, there's no call to make such a mess. We're not hiding anything from you."

"Except everything," a man says.

Mr. Harris leads me to sit on a log that we never sit on since it would crush down the grass and show that people live here. I look back to where they are talking to Father.

"Don't worry about him," Mr. Harris says. "He'll be all right. What we are going to do here is worry about you."

"Lettuce and beans growing over here," one man says. "That's really something. Check it out."

Everything is getting beaten down so it will take a long time to get it straight again so it looks like no person has walked here, like no one lives here. Father at least is still only stepping on the white stones. His voice is the calmest of all of them, the softest and deepest. I can see Randy still on the mattress, the black chess pieces against the white sheet. It's so strange to see Father's pack on someone else's back. It makes the policeman look small. He adjusts the straps, keeps bouncing it up to make it comfortable. Next to my hand on the log ants are going into tiny holes. I am so much smaller than everyone around me. My fingers are thin and can circle my wrist. I am not strong enough to change what is happening.

"This is a very unusual day for me," Mr. Harris says. He takes off his wire glasses and blinks his small eyes while he rubs the glasses with his handkerchief.

"It's only the two of you," he says. "Correct?"

"Who else would there be?" I say. "What's going to happen?"

"There will be time for more questions," he says. "I'm sorry. I see that this is a surprising time for you. A lot is changing all at once."

"Sir!" a man shouts and then they are holding Father back, who has gotten close to where I am sitting.

"Caroline," he says. "Don't be afraid. Just because they don't understand us doesn't mean we've done anything wrong. I love you. We'll be back together soon."

"Yes," I say, and a policeman puts a hand on his arm and turns Father away and then they walk away. The man with the pack and another in front, then Father, then the camouflage man with his gun pointing at the ground.

Father looks back only one time and smiles at me. I watch the back of his head slowly disappear down the slope, his hair sticking up on one side and I'm thinking it's almost time for me to cut it again.

Two

ONCE FATHER IS GONE the air around our house gets harder to breathe. I am trying to slow down my breathing. Mr. Harris and Officer Stannard are just standing there waiting for me to do or say something.

"Can I fill up my pack, too?" I say.

"Yes," Mr. Harris says. "Do you have library books, as well?"

I walk over and take my pack and put in all the papers of my journal and I pick Randy up off the mattress.

"That's quite an unusual horse," Mr. Harris says, and I tie my strip of blue ribbon around Randy's neck and push him all the way in so he's out of sight because these people don't deserve to see him.

I take out the E encyclopedia and open it to as far as I've gotten. All alone I know the E will be useless so I slide it back in with its friends. Instead I put the dictionary in my pack even though I can already tell it will be frustrating to read.

When I start putting my clothes in Mr. Harris says, "You won't need those. We can give you new clothes."

"When am I coming back?" I say.

"We have to get going," Officer Stannard says. "Take what you need, please."

"Don't rush her," Mr. Harris says.

"Will someone bring my encyclopedias?" I say.

"Not today."

I put the branch across the door to our house when I have everything I can take.

"Don't worry about that, now," Mr. Harris says with his hand on my shoulder.

"People will take all our pots," I say, "and plates and our stove and our bed even."

"Don't worry about any of that," he says. "Really. Wouldn't you like to wear shoes?"

"If you like," I say. "I can wear shoes if we're going to the city."

And then we start walking down the slope toward the soft roar of the highways. Mr. Harris is ahead of me, his arms stiff and his shoes sliding in the long grass. The way he goes leaves so many marks you would think ten people had walked here.

"Is my father waiting for us down here?" I say.

We come out of the trees and way off to the left I see the sharp green towers of the St. Johns Bridge far away and I feel those sharp inside. Straight ahead and closer is one empty black-and-white police car. Everyone else is gone. A semi-truck rattles past without slowing down.

Mr. Harris opens the back door and I sit down and swing my legs inside and he closes the door then walks around and gets in next to me. Officer Stannard is in the driver's seat. He starts the engine and we slide fast onto the road with everything passing in the window. The electrical station, Fat Cobra Video, the waste depot where sometimes we scavenged. I look behind us and it's a yellow truck. I can't see any of the other police cars or the truck the dogs probably went in, none of the places Father might be.

"You can talk," Mr. Harris says. "Or not talk, if you want to. If you want to, you can cry."

A sign says Wood Monsters. There are semi trailers on train cars and storage containers out in the railyard. In my pack on the seat between us are the things they let me bring. A cup and a jar of raisins and the dictionary and Randy, who I unzip the zipper to touch his head. I almost want to cry but I remember what Father said and I don't want them to think anything untrue.

"Did you read the scratched leaves?" I say. "The ones I scratched? That's how you found us."

"Pardon me?" Mr. Harris says.

"Nothing," I say.

We're driving toward the tall buildings. Next to us on the right is still the forest park and we drive so fast it's a blur of green. I can't see the edges of the trees, can't hardly read the signs on the road as they slide past. Machines cause more problems than they solve and I have not been riding inside a car for a very long time. For a moment I remember driving with my foster parents, sitting in the backseat like this with my little sister. Each of us is eating one half of a sweet, cold orange popsicle. Outside the windows a cemetery full of jagged gray stones stretches up a hill.

"All right," Mr. Harris says. "We're almost here. No reason to be afraid. We're just going to ask you some questions so we can decide what is the best thing to do next."

"Yes," I say. "I know that you don't understand us."

People walk up and down the streets. They cross in front of

us staring in when we stop at the red light and maybe it's because of seeing a girl in a police car. The buildings all around are tall and full of windows. The car I'm in turns across the sidewalk and drives into, under a building and past many parked cars, most of them police cars and we circle around and finally stop at a lighted door. The first thing they do once I step out of the car is take away my pack with all my things in it.

THE BUILDING is full of doors. Hallways full of closed doors where there are rooms I cannot see into. In the hallways there is nothing but adults. The floors are hard and the air smells like chemicals. I sneeze and no one blesses me.

"My name is Jean," Miss Jean Bauer says. "You can call me Jean. I work with Jim. Mr. Harris."

She has a stripe of gray hair in front but she is not old. She is only a little taller than me and she wears a white jacket with her name on it in red thread. All different colored pens are in the pocket of her jacket.

"Is Mr. Harris your boss?" I say.

"No," she says. "We work together. We just thought it would be easier for you to talk to me, maybe. But if you want to talk with him you can."

"That's all right," I say, but I'm not angry with Mr. Harris. He doesn't know any better. He doesn't understand. There is never a reason not to be polite, I know. To let someone make you angry is always a mistake. I remember this. I can tell that this building is a place to be careful.

"First we're going to have you take a shower," Miss Jean Bauer says, "and after that a quick checkup to see if you're all right and then we'll see how you're feeling. The shower is in here," she says, opening a door for me. "There's a towel and soap right there."

"You're going to watch me?" I say.

"No," she says. "I'll be back in five minutes. I'll wait right out here in the hall."

It is a large room with flickering lights. Most of it is full of gray metal lockers, some with round combination locks and some dented. There are benches made of wood and metal. The first thing I do is circle the whole room. There is one other door but it is locked closed. I decide to wait, to do what they say. Father could be close in this building. There are so many doors, so many rooms.

It is not just one shower but almost a little room with ten showers sticking out of the tiled walls and the floor is tile too with metal drains in it. There's water drops under one shower and I decide that's where Father was, right before me. Whatever they want to do with us they want us to be very clean.

I want to turn all of the showers on at once but the handles are tight and my hands are small. The water is so hot and then I remember and turn the other handle to mix the cold. It's so different than in the forest park where usually we use a shower made out of a silver bag that we hang up high in a tree so the water gets warm and no one sees it. This is a ways from our camp, a good walk we walk carrying our clean clothes. We bring the shower down with me usually climbing the tree and there is gallons of water but it goes fast. So first we strip down and turn it on enough to get wet, second we soap up, third we rinse off. Twice a week or less in the winter when it's cold. In the summer sometimes we use the water cold. Sometimes when it rains we find a place where the trees aren't thick and we strip down there and soap up and rinse off in the hard rain.

It is so different in the building, in the tiled room with ten showers. The water keeps coming and coming, never running out and through it I can hear someone calling my name. I step out of the water coming down with water still in my ears.

"Finish up," Miss Jean Bauer says from where I can't see her. "It's been ten minutes."

The towel is so soft and when I get back to my clothes my clothes are gone and on a hanger is a dress that has only two ties and is made of paper.

"Where are my things?" I say. "I need a comb. Where's Randy?"

"Who's Randy?" Miss Jean Bauer says. "Just put on that robe; I'll give you clothes after what we do next."

"What am I going to do next?" I say.

She bends down a little to look at my face. "How are you holding up?" she says.

"What do you mean?" I say.

"Aren't you tired? You must be exhausted."

"Why?" I say. "I've hardly done anything at all today."

She asks if it's all right if she stays in the room once we've reached the Doctor's room and then stands there with a clipboard sometimes writing and sometimes listening.

None of it really surprises me except that I am now five feet three inches and ninety-seven pounds, almost a hundred. It's been a long time since I've been measured or weighed.

The Doctor has no hair on his head. He shines lights in my

ears and nose and mouth. He looks at my teeth. He listens to my heart and organs with a stethoscope.

"Do you have any pains?" he says. "Any part of your body that's hurting you?"

"No," I say. "Would you like to see me run?"

He bends down and looks into my vagina with his light. I explain menstruation to him and Miss Jean Bauer writes down some of what I say.

"All it really means is that a girl is ready for breeding," I say, "but I'm not to do that until I'm twenty at least and married."

"I see," the Doctor says, and says I can get dressed. "I'm very happy to report that you're an extremely healthy young woman," he says, "who's really taken care of herself."

"Father teaches me," I say.

THE CLOTHES Miss Jean Bauer gives me are blue pants that are too short and a blue buttoned shirt that is scratchy and doesn't match. There's new white underpants and white socks. All that is left are my black city shoes.

"I am also supposed to wear an undershirt," I say, but she doesn't seem to hear me as she walks ahead of me.

The next room is full of wooden chairs that have desks attached like a kind of arm on the right side. There are blackboards but no writing on them and no chalk in the metal trays. I sit down in the front row.

"Are any other children coming?" I say.

"No," Miss Jean Bauer says. "Just you." She hands me a pencil and a booklet of paper and then some scratch paper. "Can you read?" she says. "If not, that's fine. I can read it for you."

"Of course I can read," I say.

"I'll be just outside," she says. "If you need me."

The questions are sometimes like stories and then you have to mark what they meant or why someone did something or what they should do. Or simpler ones about what tools are for what or what is a shelter and what is not a shelter. It's kind of fun. It keeps me from thinking of other things. I want to get all the questions all correct in case that will help. The math hardly gets up to algebra but still I double-check my answers on the scratch paper.

After half an hour the door opens a little and Miss Jean Bauer looks in at me and I look up from writing and she closes the door without saying anything. After another half hour I am finished and I'm using the pencil to pull the snarls out of my hair which is now mostly dry and then the door opens again.

"How's it coming?" she says. "Are you taking a break?"

"I'm done," I say.

"Already? Are you sure?" She has three silver rings on each hand and she turns through the pages of the booklet.

"Yes," I say.

"Yes you are," she says.

"It's like homework," I say. "Only easier."

"When did you have homework?" she says.

"All the time," I say. "Is this place a school? For adults, maybe?"

"That's very smart," she says. "These are rooms where police officers sometimes get trained or take classes."

"How many rooms are in this building?" I say.

"I don't know that," she says.

"It's a big one, though," I say. "How many people are inside?"

"Yes," she says. "It's big."

"Am I going to live here?" I say.

"No," she says, and smiles. "Do you understand why you're here?"

"I would like please to be back together with Father," I say.

"Let me explain a few things to you, Caroline," she says. "So you'll understand. A person running in the park saw you last week, and it is illegal, against the law for people to live in the park but especially we had to check out the report of a young girl. To see if you wanted to be there, or who took you there, to make sure that you were all right."

"You chased us with dogs," I say.

"We're trying to help," she says. "We're trying to get a complete picture of the situation."

"The way we live is different," I say, "than how you are used to things being."

"Very true," Miss Jean Bauer says.

She looks at her watch and I see that it says four thirty and I look at mine which says eleven twenty. I think of my father somewhere with the same time on his watch.

"Let's see," she says. "You must be hungry. It's a few hours to lights-out and then tomorrow morning you and I can talk some more."

THIS ROOM HAS a round table and on one side two bunk beds and on the other side a green chair and a plaid couch with sagging cushions and a television that two girls are watching. When they turn to look I see that one is Valerie from the Skeleton Family so I run over and touch her arm.

"It's me," I say. "Where are we?"

"We're locked up," she says. Her hair is all bleached white and cut ragged at her shoulders. She has six earrings in one ear and five in the other and a ring pierced between her nostrils. Her lips are all chapped and dry from licking them.

"Taffy," she says to the other girl, "this is the chick I told you about before, that girl that lives in Forest Park."

"I do not," I say.

"With her father," she says.

"We have a house but we spend a lot of time in the forest park," I say. "Because we like it."

"Right," she says. "You sleep there."

"A couple times," I say. "Just to go camping. You don't know where I'm from."

"Whatever," Valerie says. "This is Taffy."

They are both wearing the same outfit as I have on only Valerie has dirty sneakers and Taffy has on rubber sandals. Taffy has what looks like blue ballpoint pen scribbled on her cheek and forehead. She's even skinnier than Valerie, with dark hair longer on one side.

"Is that your real name?" I say.

"Yes," she says.

"That's really nice," Valerie says. "That's a really nice way to be. You see how she is, Taffy, growing up in the woods so she has no manners."

"I do so," I say. "I just never heard that name before."

There is no room on the sofa so I try to sit on the edge of the green chair which is cold and slippery.

"Why are you here?" I say.

"Shoplifting," Valerie says. "Taking spray paint and whipped cream for whip-its."

"What?" I say. "Did Johnny and Isabel tell you to steal?"

"Duh," she says.

"How long have you been here?" I say.

"These fuckers have no idea about my parents," she says, "or how a real family works. Johnny and Isabel know."

"Have you seen my father here?" I say.

"Maybe," Valerie says, "just maybe you got luckier with your daddy but you see how this shit works out so the police will try to take you apart from your family every time."

"Right," Taffy says. She is looking at me but still watching the television where a woman in a dress is shouting at and then kissing a man in a doctor's uniform.

"Now stop interrupting," Valerie says, "so we can watch our show."

After a minute I go over and look at the bunk beds.

"That one is ours," Valerie says, pointing and shouting. "Don't touch it. You take the other one."

There's only one window and it looks across to a brick wall. Down below is only an alley with no one in it except a trash can and what looks like the broken part of a bicycle. If I lean close to the glass I can see only a long thin line of sky which is barely blue.

The voices on the television are loud and ridiculous. Everyone is very excited. I want to watch it and I don't want to watch it. I start walking circles around the room, right close to the walls. The window, a corner, behind the television, a corner, past the door, a corner around the beds. The fourth time around I kick the cord out of the wall and Valerie and Taffy yell and I only look at the plug before Valerie leaps up and sticks it into the wall and leaps back to the couch so she won't miss anything.

"Jesus," she says. "Retarded."

I sit at the table and try to remember the game we'd played in the forest park on one of the few times Father let me. Something about driving a car and to a beach and the kitten was part of the game but now I'm afraid to say anything about that since she seems so angry and is watching the television. I wait until the show is over and then I try to talk again.

"I like your hair," I say.

"No you don't," Valerie says. "What a fake thing to say."

"What do you think Nameless is doing right now?" I say.

"That idiot," she says. "Probably eating bugs or worms or something."

"I don't know if he really does that," I say. "At least he's not in here. He didn't get caught."

"Not yet," she says.

"What happened to your kitten?" I say.

"He's gone away somewhere," she says. "Probably the same place as that dumb horse of yours."

Later I take the top bunk and Valerie is in the other top bunk straight across from me in the dark. She is whispering to Taffy and Taffy whispers back and it's in a way where I can't understand the words.

"What are you saying?" I say, and they giggle and after a while start up again.

I wonder how many days it will be and if that will be long enough for all three of us to be friends together. I cannot fall asleep in the same room with them and without Father next to me. I stretch my foot all across the bed and don't touch his hairy leg. I rest there with my foot sticking out in the air until it's cold and I pull it back. Somewhere I hear a dog barking far away. I am thinking hard on Father's face so hard that I can feel him thinking back at me and so I don't worry. Miss Jean Bauer said it was illegal to live in the forest park and I wonder if already Father is in an orange outfit, if he'll be taken out to cut the long grass with the white truck of dogs watching him through their cages, ready to chase.

A WIZARD IS ONE who practices magic but can also be a person who is clever at a task or test, which is a series of questions, a trial, affliction, crucible, ordeal, tribulation, visitation.

WE SIT ON SOFT CHAIRS in Miss Jean Bauer's office. She has flowers and a computer. Out the window I can see more tall buildings of the city. She scoots closer and touches my arm with her hand.

"Now Caroline," she says, "how was your breakfast?"

"I liked the orange juice," I say.

"Good. Now is it all right if I ask you a few questions?"

"Yes," I say. "That's what you said we were going to do."

"Your name is Caroline and you are a thirteen-year-old girl who has been living with your father. Correct?"

"Where is Father?" I say.

"He's close," she says. "He's fine. He's doing fine. He misses you, too."

"Can I see him?" I say. "Of course that's my name."

"We just want to make certain we have everything right," she says, "so we can start."

"If I scream," I say, "would he hear me?"

"Please don't scream."

"I wouldn't scream," I say. "There's never any good reason to raise one's voice."

"Really?" she says. "Why do you think that?"

"When will I see my Father?" I say.

"Your physical and mental examinations have been very good," she says. "Excellent, in fact. Would you say you've had a happy and normal childhood?"

"Am I going to stay here forever?" I say.

"No," she says. "Don't worry. I've told you that before. Let's try it this way: I'll say what your father told me and you can tell me if it's not right, okay? He says that you lived in Forest Park for four years because it was safer and better for you than being on the streets and he didn't have the money to rent an apartment or a house. He says you've never met your mother, that she passed away?"

"We have a house," I say. "My father is paid every month. She had the same name as me."

"Caroline."

"Yes."

"But you haven't gone to school," she says.

"My father teaches me at our house," I say. "You said I passed your test, so we should be able to go back home."

"Yes," she says, "you're ahead of where you need to be, but

you must understand that you can't live there. And school is about social skills, too, not only intellectual ones."

"I am happy," I say. "I was happy. Where are the dogs?"

"Who?" she says.

"The dogs who found us. Are they here?"

"In this building?" she says. "No. They are search and rescue dogs."

"Are they the ones who watch the criminals?" I say.

"They live in kennels," she says, "at the police station."

"We didn't need to be rescued," I say.

I like Miss Jean Bauer and I like the gray streak in her hair but I don't say this. I can tell she likes me even if she doesn't understand me.

"Is that picture your husband?" I say.

"My boyfriend," she says.

"He's handsome."

"Yes, he is," she says.

"Do you have a daughter?" I say.

"No, I don't."

"Do you have a father that you can see and hear and talk to?" I say.

She touches my hand again and says, "It's amazing to me, Caroline, the life you've had so far. Not many people can tell a story like that and now there's so many new opportunities for you. Still," she says, "I wish I could have just followed you around for a day, just to see how you did it all."

"You wouldn't have been able to follow me," I say. "I'd lose you in five minutes. Even with dogs it might not matter."

"Did you grow all the food you ate?" she said. "Your father says you're vegetarians."

"No," I say. "Yes we are vegetarians but we went to Safeway, too. Everyone goes to a store, or eats things they find in the city that other people leave behind."

"Did you take things from other people?"

"Never," I say. "If someone in the forest park drops something, the rule is to wait and count to thirty. Then you can pick it up. Hide. Count again to fifty, to see if anyone comes back. If they do, try to put it in their path a little further along, so they can find it and so you won't be stealing from them."

"So you went to Safeway every two weeks?" she says.

"Everyone has to buy something sometime," I say. "Only maybe Nameless only eats what grows in the forest park."

"Who's that?" she says. "A friend of yours?"

"Not exactly," I say. "It doesn't matter. Is Father somewhere taking tests like this?"

"Kind of," she says. "They've been asking him a lot of questions. He's been very cooperative."

"We're different than you," I say.

"We're just deciding what is the best thing to do," she says again. "You can see that we have to understand where you've been and who you are, first."

I don't know what to say so I just look out the window again. I button the button on the cuff of the shirt they gave me.

"Please," I say. "I don't know what to say. Those are all the things I can think of. Can I not go in with those girls again?"

"Is there a problem?" she says.

"There's not even any books in there," I say. "I can't breathe. I can't even see one tree out the window."

"We don't want to make a mistake," she says. "How about this? How about we try something new?"

She takes out a bright blue box then, thin but as tall and wide as a piece of paper. From a drawer she pulls out a square machine with black and red buttons on it.

"I am wondering if it's all right if I make a tape recording of our conversation," she says. "Would that be all right? If you like, I can give you a copy of the tape to keep."

"All right," I say. "But I already said I'm out of things to say."

Miss Jean Bauer pushes down the red button and I can see the wheels turning inside the clear plastic window. She picks up the blue box again and takes off the top.

"This is a storytelling test," she says. "Actually, it's more like a game. Think of it like a game. I have some pictures here that I am going to show you, and for each picture I want you to make up a story. Tell what has happened before and what is happening now. Say what the people are feeling and thinking and how it will come out. You can make up any kind of story you please. Do you understand? Well, then, get ready for your first picture. You have five minutes to make up a story. See how well you can do."

This takes an hour almost. She keeps telling me if I have more time or if I'm running out even if I can see the minutes going on my watch. The pictures are not easy. There's a woman coming through a door with her face down in her hand and men asleep on the grass resting with their heads on each other and hats over their eyes and one where a girl in a tree watches another girl in a dress running along a beach and holding up her dress out of the waves. I tell stories for them and mostly Miss Jean Bauer tells me they're good stories. The first one is a picture of a boy and a violin and this is the story I tell:

"There's a spider down in the violin and then he's sitting there wondering if it's going to come out of it and if it will bite his chin if he begins to play. But his mind keeps drifting away so he's not worried."

"Where is his mind drifting?" she says. "What's he thinking about?"

"He wants to go outside, I think."

"And what will happen?"

"He'll probably play that violin for a while and the spider will just listen," I say. "How do you read my answers? You think they mean in a certain way, but how do you know?"

"Don't worry about any of that," she says. "Just tell me the first story that comes in your mind. Have you ever seen an X ray?"

"Yes," I say. "I know what one is."

"Well," she says, "we're trying to find out what it looks like inside you, by the stories you tell."

"You could just ask," I say.

"Yes, but you might not be able to say it."

"So it's a crooked way you're going," I say. "So I'll somehow say what I can't say."

"Right," she says. "That's not a bad way to think about it." And then she shows me a picture of a person turned away with their head on a bench and a gun on the floor and then another with a woman on a couch reading a book to a girl holding a doll and looking away like she might not be listening.

IT IS SO HARD to be in the room with these girls. I sit at the round table with the pencil and scratch paper trying to write and then I get up and stand next to the window and I feel like breaking the glass in that room since it seems like it should be easier to breathe and I can't get air. Every time the door opens I think it could be Father and I look up and instead it's Miss Jean Bauer or Mr. Harris coming to get me or Valerie or Taffy.

My feet hurt so I take off my shoes and put the socks inside them. The floor is too hard and smooth beneath my feet. It's cold. The air smells like all the chemicals it takes to keep everything so clean.

"Gross," Valerie says. "You're getting your dirty feet all over everything."

"My feet are clean," I say.

"You act like you're better than everyone. Different."

"That's not true," I say to her even if what she says makes me think that I do feel that way but I don't act that way.

"What's your problem?" she says.

"I don't have a problem."

"That's your problem," she says. "That you think you're so great and don't have any problems. And your watch is always the wrong time. Stupid."

"My problem is that I got taken away from my father," I say. "Obviously. And then I got locked in here where you're trying to argue with me."

"I can ask whatever I want," she says, "if you have a problem. Is it me? Is that what you're saying?"

"This is such a dumb conversation," I say. "I used to think we were almost friends and now we only talk like this, not saying anything at all."

Taffy sits watching the television and then turning her head, looking at Valerie and then looking at me. Listening. Her face is happy like she expects something.

"You think I'm dumb?" Valerie says. "You don't even have any friends."

"I do," I say. "I have a friend named Zachary."

"Is he your boyfriend?"

"No," I say.

"Is Richard your boyfriend?" she says. "Do you think that?"

"Richard? No. He tried to give me a bracelet but I didn't accept it."

"Bitch," she says, standing close to push my shoulder. "Richard is my boyfriend," she says. "Don't you ever touch him. Don't even say his name again. What are you laughing at?"

"I was thinking about Zachary," I say. "He believes in Bigfoot but really it's only Nameless."

"Whatever," Valerie says, and then reaches out to grab at me and tries to slap but is too slow and then she's chasing me around the table and is already breathing hard. She curses and picks up a chair and throws it over the table and I leap so it hits the wall and crashes down next to me. She comes around and I swing another chair loose from under the table and push it hard sliding so it hits her knees and knocks her down and right away I'm over her. When she tries to stand I push her back to the floor.

"Stop," I say. I put my hand on her neck.

"Bitch," she says, after a while, once she's crawled over the couch where Taffy's been watching. "Bitch," Valerie says, rubbing her neck. "I'm not talking to you again. I'm never going to be your friend now."

IT IS IMPORTANT to always remember that at any time you think of it there are people being kept in buildings when they want to go outside.

"I'M GOING TO SHOW YOU ten pictures again," Miss Jean Bauer says.

"Were there ten the first time?"

"Yes."

She pushes down the red button on the tape recorder.

"I didn't keep count," I say.

She takes out the blue box and a booklet and she is partly talking and partly reading to me.

"It will be easier for you this time," she says, "because the pictures I have here are much better, more interesting. You told me some fine stories the other day. Now I want to see whether you make up a few more. Make them even more exciting than you did last time if you can. Like a dream or fairy tale. Here's the first picture."

"There's snow all around a house," I say, "and the two windows are like round eyes since there's lights on where it's warm I think and it's cold outside and frozen and windy. And there you can see a black kind of ghost swirling over the roof by the chimney with two eyes and up there there might be another ghost but that might be another ghost or it could just be another cloud about to snow some more. It's cold. The snow there in the front is drifted and frozen up like a jagged kind of wing."

"Do you believe in ghosts?" she says.

"Yes," I say.

"Have you ever seen a ghost?"

"I don't know," I say.

"So," she says and touches my hand. "If a stick leaps up and strikes you or if you see a stone rolling uphill, is that a ghost that does that?"

"You've been reading my journal," I say. "That's not right. That's not a polite thing to do at all. Where is my backpack and my things?"

"You'll get them back," Miss Jean Bauer says. "And I'm being careful, I just am trying to figure things out. Your writing is beautiful. You should keep writing, Caroline."

"Most of that is homework, anyway," I say.

"We know," she says. "It's very impressive."

"And Randy?" I say.

"Who?"

"My horse," I say. "You shouldn't be reading my journal."

We sit still and not talking and our faces looking at each other without saying anything. I am not going to talk first. Miss Jean Bauer's mouth is smiling the smallest smile and at last it shifts and then moves.

"So far," she says, "you've really only described the picture. Remember, I want you to tell a story. What is happening? Are there people in this picture whom we cannot see, Caroline?"

I look at the picture on the card and I know that fighting with Miss Jean Bauer will not help me.

"There are two people inside that house who are sitting next to a fire and they're warm and maybe playing chess together. They can hear the whistle of the wind and maybe that ghost hugging down on the roof but they're safe in there. They get up and look out the window at the storm since it's scary and beautiful and everything that they need they have even if the storm keeps up. They are listening and trying to hear what the ghost is talking about and he is saying I wish I had fur all over my body and I was a person too who died and his words are all frozen and slick. Or it could be that the house is out in the storm and there are cold people lost in the snow and scared. Their feet are almost frozen off and their faces hurt from being cold and they are almost crawling because of the deep snow and one looks up at the lights and sees the house. But they see the ghosts too. Or what it is is that the first people look out, see in that window maybe that's someone looking out by the blurry curtain and see the frozen people crawling in the snow and they call out to them and maybe get a sled. By the fire their clothes melt until they can take them off and they get dry clothes. And soup. Even they can get up then and look out the window at the storm and the frozen wing in the yard."

OUTSIDE OF MISS JEAN BAUER'S office I turn right, back toward the room with Valerie and Taffy but Miss Jean Bauer says, "No, Caroline, come this way."

We go down a long hallway, up a flight of stairs and around

two corners, in a door and across a dark empty basketball court and into another hallway. I try to keep track of the turns to know the way back even if I don't want to go back.

"Wait here," she says. "One moment." She takes out a key and opens a door and goes in while I'm still in the hallway. I drink out of a water fountain and the water is so cold it hurts my teeth.

Miss Jean Bauer comes out holding something in her hand and that something is Randy. I don't say anything until he's in my hand and my fingers touch his shape that they know, the edges of his organs and his sharp ears and his numbers slightly raised up and sticky. I want to look at him but I don't want her watching me. I unbutton two buttons on my shirt and slide him inside and button it up so I can feel his plastic body against my skin there.

"Thank you," I say.

"We really want it to work out," she says. "We want to try something we haven't done before and we don't know if it will work so you'll have to help us. We can trust you to help us, right?"

"What are you talking about?" I say.

"I brought you a book to read, too," she says. "It's one I like. The first time I read it I was your age."

The book is small and blue with a dragon on it. I don't read the title since I'm watching where we're walking again, not back the way we came.

"Did anyone go back for my encyclopedias?" I say.

"I don't know," she says. "I don't think so, to be honest. I don't think you'll need them anymore."

"What?" I say.

"What would you think about going to a regular school?" she says. "In the fall, when it starts up again."

"Father can teach me," I say.

"But you can have friends your own age. Wouldn't you like that?"

"Sometimes I think so," I say, "and other times I think I wouldn't."

We pass an ax inside a glass window and a lighted machine for soft drinks. Miss Jean Bauer takes out another key and opens another door so I can go inside. She doesn't follow me.

THIS ROOM IS my own room. My paper and pencil and the sweater they gave me, the things from the other room have been brought into this small room. It only holds one bed and I go straight across to the window. Through it I can see over the rail-yard and all the trains and metal to the forest park. The sun is almost sliding behind it so all the thick trees are dark gray but still I know it and it's not so far away. In the morning I know the sun will be shining on it and then it will be green.

Also this window even opens, only five inches and there are metal locks but still I can breathe even if I can't get out so high above. I turn my head sideways and force it tight as far through as it will go.

"Hello," I say, softly, just in case. I close my eyes and think of the shadows in the trees and wonder again about the dogs and if they knew what they were doing and if they're sorry now.

I am not happy but I have Randy and the fresh air. I check the door and it's locked and then I sit down on the bed since there's no chair in the room. I take off my shoes and the scratchy shirt.

I am getting used to the smell of the soap they give me in this building and I'm not happy that I am.

The book that Miss Jean Bauer gave me does have dragons in it. It has strange weather and animals I've never heard of and spells that keep things from falling apart. It is about a wizard who I like and I copy out part of it on my scratch paper:

> From that time forth he believed that the wise man is one who never sets himself apart from other living things, whether they have speech or not, and in later years he strove long to learn what can be learned, in silence, from the eyes of animals, the flight of birds, the great slow gestures of trees.

It has been a long time since I read a book like this one, a story instead of a book of facts. It has maps in it of islands I've never heard of, like two called The Hands that look like hands. The boy in it starts out by talking to goats and then gets more and more power. He learns from trees and birds and animals, like I copied down. I read until I have to turn on the light to keep reading and I do until it's late at night and I am reaching the end. The wizard in this book is called Sparrowhawk but that is not his real name. Almost no one knows his real name. The magic in this place is all about naming, knowing the real name of a thing or person. Then you can control them. And a thing can be changed into another thing as long as it is renamed and the spell lasts.

Three

FATHER STANDS ON the sidewalk next to a police car. He doesn't see me at first. His arms are loose and not held behind him. He wears stiff new blue jeans and a light blue shirt. His hair is cut close and his skin shows through white above his ears. Still he recognizes the sound of my footsteps, my breath when I see him and take it in hard. He turns and picks me up, my feet off the ground and his whiskers against my forehead.

"Caroline," he says. "My heart."

I have my pack again with Randy and all my papers, my blue ribbon, my dictionary, the things I took from our house and they want to put it in the trunk with Father's red pack but I keep it with me, down by my feet in the back of the car.

That's where we ride. We drive between the buildings with cars on both sides of us. Through the windows of stores I can see jewelry and long tables and many bright lamps hanging from chains. I squeeze Father's hand more tightly and he squeezes back. I can't see between the buildings or far behind us but I feel that we're driving away from the forest park, that we're not going back there. I can't even see the river. We cross a bridge where cars speed under us and then we're in a black tunnel. In the darkness Father leans close so I can smell him and feel his face against mine. He whispers one word, my name, and is sitting up straight again before we come out the other end into the brightness, racing all the other cars up a curving slope.

"You two can talk," says the officer in the passenger seat. "Don't worry. I'm sure you have lots to say to each other."

"They don't want to talk in front of us," the driver says.

I want to know where Father was and what they asked him. I want to tell him that I passed all the tests and also about the stories I made from the pictures and the book I read.

The first officer turns to look back at us. "Aren't you even curious where we're going?" he says.

"I've heard a little about it," Father says. "A little surprise isn't a bad thing."

"You'll like it," the officer says. "I bet you'll like it."

The truth is I don't care so much about where we're going as long as we're together but I don't say this aloud. Now the city is down below, far behind us. I can see the river for a moment and then it's gone. Black crows hop along the edge of the highway. Far above a vulture is circling, watching us slide past. The seat belts have silver buckles with square metal buttons in the middle. The windows in the back have no handles to roll them down. Music comes up behind my head, the sound of violins out of a speaker. The officer driving turns the knob and it goes off with a click.

"I was thinking," Father says, "you know how sometimes a bear will move too close to a town or a ranch and they catch it or tranquilize it?"

"Yeah," the officer driving says.

"How would it be if you just let us free in a real wilderness?" Father says. "Just let us free."

"Would you like that?" the officer says. "Trust me, this'll be better."

Father is smiling in a way I haven't seen before or maybe I've forgotten. His voice seems less low. I look at him and he squeezes my hand and looks out the window like it's a natural thing for us to be inside a car, racing along the highway.

"Horses," I say when I see them. I have seen horses before but not for a long time. Some are standing beneath a tree and others are eating grass and two brown ones run powerfully along next to the fence like they're racing our car.

"You're going to like this, Caroline," one of the officers says. I didn't know he knew my name.

Just past the horses we turn at a gravel driveway and roll by two red barns. Up ahead is a tall house and a smaller building at the bottom of a slope and next to the smaller building is a car with its door open. I see as we get close that it's Miss Jean Bauer and Mr. Harris and two other men standing next to that car, waving at our car.

When we stop I open the door and set my feet down on the unmoving ground.

"Welcome," they are saying, shouting. "Welcome to your new house!"

OUR NEW HOUSE has a table and two chairs. There are two bedrooms and two beds. The bathroom has a shower and sink and a toilet and mirror. The kitchen has a refrigerator. Also it has: pots, pans, a kettle, matching plates, sharp knives that stick into slots in a wooden block. It is not a proper house but it is a

real house. It is a bunkhouse since it is where the workers lived
who worked for the man in the proper house. Mr. Walters lives
in the big house now and Father is going to work for him. This
is the job they've found for Father since we can no longer live in
the forest park.

The whole time they are showing us they are proud of themselves. I keep hold of Father's hand as they show us through all
the rooms. It is tight with all of us to get through the doorways.

"This will be so much better," Miss Jean Bauer says with her
hand on my shoulder. "Caroline will be able to start school in a
month and a half and get back to having a regular education like
any child here in Oregon."

"Yes," Father says. "Thank you for all this. Say thank you,
Caroline."

"Thank you," I say.

"We'll pay you back," Father says. "For all this. I didn't expect."

"Oh, no," Mr. Harris says. "If you want to pay us back, work
hard and keep being good to each other. Mr. Walters is a gener-
ous man," he says. "You're lucky."

"We are," I say.

Mr. Walters is short and round and very friendly. His skin is
pale white and there is no hair on his head, hardly even eyebrows.
He wears both suspenders and a belt and he stands listening to
Mr. Harris talk about him. He points things out as we go.

"I'm so excited we can do this," he says. "I've been hearing
and reading all about you and I think this could be the perfect
solution. I do need some help out here."

The other man is from the newspaper and he says hello but is already writing in his small notebook the whole time. He looks up at us and then to what he's writing. He turns a page.

"Is it all right if I take a photograph?" this man says.

"No," Father says. "No."

"A few questions?"

"I'm afraid not," Father says.

"That's all right," Mr. Harris says. "That's just fine. We all respect your privacy."

I keep looking around. In the bedroom that's mine there's a poster of a tall brown horse on the wall. The bathroom has a shower with a glass door. A back door goes out Father's room. The refrigerator holds food and there are cans in the cupboards. There's milk that isn't powder.

"Do you like it?" Miss Jean Bauer keeps asking me.

"It's too much for her to process," Mr. Harris says

After a while they have run out of things to show us.

"Tomorrow will be a full day," Mr. Walters says. "We'll go through all sorts of things tomorrow."

The police car drove away before and now the rest drive away and we turn from where we are in front of the small house and go back inside.

"It feels good to be by ourselves again," I say.

Father opens a window and breathes out.

"They had me take tests," I say. "I passed, I was ahead of where I'm supposed to be."

"Of course you were, Caroline," he says. "They wouldn't know what to do with a smart girl like you."

"And they had pictures," I say, "where I had to make up a story."

"Enough, Caroline," he says. "All of that, let's forget it happened. That tires a person out."

"But everything's different now," I say. "How we're going to live here and everything."

"It only seems different," he says. "Really it's going to be the same."

I am kicking off my shoes and balling my socks. Father goes into the kitchen and takes the tinfoil off the casserole they left then puts the tinfoil back over it. He opens the refrigerator door so the cold light shines on him and then shuts it without taking anything out.

LATER I STAND ALONE in the bedroom that is my bedroom. Through my window I can see the long slope of tall grass that leads into trees which is where the stream is and where we'll irrigate. I can also see the edge of the pasture and a corner of a corral where in the dusk I can see the dark shapes of horses. Randy rests on his side atop the dresser with my blue ribbon tied around him so I won't lose it. Beneath him in the drawers are: underpants, undershirts, socks, jeans, skirts. Blouses hang in the closet. I have a sweater and sandals and blue sneakers with blue stripes, all new.

I move Randy to the square table beside my bed so if I wake up in the night I can reach out to touch him. The lamp's switch is black plastic and turns like a key. I used to have one like it. The sheets are cold and white and the wool blanket smells like mothballs.

Under the blankets I try to sleep. The moon shines through the window and the shadows breathe. I can hear animals scratching somewhere but I cannot see them. Crickets outside are also breathing together. I can almost not believe how lucky we are and at the same time we do not feel like us at all. The face of my watch glows round but I cannot see the hands right. Has an hour passed? Two hours? I open the covers with a slap and set my bare feet on the ridges of the rug. I step across it and across the cold linoleum of the bathroom, into the darker hall. I open the door and step through into Father's room where the air is clearer to see.

"Is it all right?" I say, caught between the door and the bed.

"Oh, girl," Father says, just holding up the sheet and blanket so I can slide underneath. "I was going to come in there," he says, his mouth close to my ear. "We can't do every single thing the way they want us to. That's how we are."

"We're smarter than they are," I say.

"Yes," he says, "but we have to be smart enough so they don't know that."

"So they can think they're smarter?"

"Exactly," he says.

My breath slows now. Father's hairy legs are soft against mine under the covers. Through all the new smells he still smells like himself and lying still like this we feel like ourselves again. When he shifts the blankets his bracelets clink together and I am happy to hear the sound.

"I couldn't sleep either," he says. "I couldn't hardly sleep at all, these last five days. I'm sorry." He kisses my forehead. "I'm so sorry, Caroline. It's all my fault," he says. "We stayed in the last camp too long, but it was such a good one, I thought."

I don't say anything but I think of my shirt in the tree's branches, that I took off to look at my body and that the runner saw so that our house was found and we were caught.

FATHER ISN'T IN BED when I wake up. He is looking out the window looking at the sky. He is not standing in front of the window but next to it so someone outside wouldn't see him there.

"What is it?" I say.

"Nothing," he says. "Good morning, Caroline. Aren't you curious what's been provided for our breakfast?"

We have not only real milk but real orange juice at breakfast. Cold cereal named Cheerios and Chex.

"Can you believe all this is ours?" I say. "This whole house."

"To keep bright the devil's doorknobs and scour his tubs," Father says. "Better not to keep a house."

"What?" I say, and then there's a knocking. It's Mr. Walters.

"Good morning," he says, opening the door. "Don't mean to interrupt your breakfast."

"Not at all." Father stands and walks to the doorway.

"I know from reading about you in the paper that you have your particular ways," Mr. Walters says, "and I don't want to cause any discomfort."

"We're just finishing," Father says. "What do you have planned for us today?"

"I was hoping you could take the tractor down to the south pasture," Mr. Walters says, "and drag some brush out from around the water tank. I'll show you where I'm talking about."

"I'd rather work with the horses," Father says. "Down in the stables."

"Yes, but I'd rather you not work down there. Mostly it's the ladies who come to see their horses and to ride. They're used to things being a certain way. They're wealthy ladies, mostly."

"I won't even talk to them," Father says. "I won't look at them. I'd just rather not drive the tractors or trucks."

"What are you," Mr. Walters says, "some kind of Mennonite? Or do you not know how?"

"No, I'm not," Father says, "and I do know how."

"Remember," Mr. Walters says, "I'm doing you a favor here. Things could go a really different way if you don't want to cooperate."

It's quiet for a little while. I can see blue sky around Father's head where he stands in the open doorway. A cloud disappears behind his shoulders. I cannot see Mr. Walters at all.

"Okay," Father says. "I don't forget how you're putting yourself out for us. Tractors, trucks, snowplows, whatever. I can drive them all."

FROM THAT FIRST DAY Mr. Walters is trying to separate us, saying I don't have to be so close to Father while he works, that I'll get in the way, that it's dangerous. Still I stay close. I play in the long grass. I climb trees and watch Father work and it is not dangerous and I do not get in the way. I help him. We move manure. We fix window screens. We rub saddles and bridles with saddle soap until they shine and my fingers are sticky for days. We stretch the barbed-wire fences tighter and mend where the wire is broken. My arms are lined with scabs and my jeans are snagged from the barbs.

My favorite job is irrigating. Not moving the metal pipes out

on the flat pastures which are too heavy for me but irrigating
where Father and I both wear tall black rubber boots and over
his shoulder he has a sharp square shovel and an orange plastic
tarp wrapped around a wooden post. At the stream I pull the
tarp unwinding and then he lays the post across the stream and
we take heavy stones and weight the tarp down underwater. He
cuts with the shovel pieces of sod to block the water better even
though we have to let some past so it flows down to the next
farm. We share. But our dam spills water mostly down over the
slope into the grass all the way almost to our bunkhouse. We
move the dam twice a day and the grass grows in wedges that
are green where we've already been. It shows how long we've
been here.

Up close to the stream is a stand of aspens that are loud in the
wind and that I climb. From them I can see our house and my
bedroom window and I know Randy is safe inside on the dresser.
I can see the horses out in their corrals and pastures. There is no
direction to look where there is not a road or building.

"I like it here," I say. "Don't you like it?"

"They want you to like it," Father says. "This way they can
know where you are at all times."

"Who?" I say. "What?"

Father wears a straw hat on his head since we cannot stay in
the shade like we used to and most of the trees have been cut
down on the farm a long time ago. The sun still finds its way
through the woven straw, sliding yellow needles down around
Father's eyes and the skin of his cheeks as he stands with the
muddy water sliding around his black boots. He points down to
the road half a mile away, his head turning to follow each car.

"You see how they slow down as they pass?" he says. "And look at the size of these ladies' trucks. Who would need a truck like that?"

The wealthy ladies are riding their horses. Horses smell thicker than I expected them to. Dustier. But it's okay and they hardly make me sneeze after the first few times.

The ladies are beautiful. They ride with their backs straight and their whips in one hand. They wear tall black leather boots and white shirts buttoned up tight to their necks. Their hair is usually blond and straight and swings when they corner or jump a jump. They wear black helmets in case they fall but they never fall. They circle for the next jump and lean down to pat their horses' long necks. They whisper into their horses' sharp ears.

I HAVE NEVER SEEN a helicopter up close, only far away over the river and the freeway hovering over the colored lines of traffic. In the war, Father says, the blades of the helicopters which are called rotors spit sand in everyone's eyes and whipped their hair around. The helicopters rose up and came down and chopped branches off trees. They brought injured bodies and threw out papers to tell living people what to do next. Ever since I've known him Father has dreamed of helicopters and they come thick in these nights on the farm. He cries out and kicks and wakes up and I wake up to gentle him, talking about other things and talking him around to where I want to go while he is still sweating and slowing down.

"If you could be any animal," I say. "What would you be?"

"Not a horse," Father says. "Definitely not a horse. Maybe a bird."

"What kind?"

"Any kind that could fly," he says. "A small bird, but not a hummingbird."

"Why not?"

"Too much sugar," he says. "Too weird, all that darting around."

"Horses," I say. "Did my mother ride horses?"

"How did you guess that?" he says.

"And that's why you got me Randy?"

"Partly. Yes."

I pull up the sheet and fold the top up over the blanket so it won't be rough on our faces.

"In the building," I say, "they talked to me about mother, they asked questions. They wanted to know if I remembered her."

"Your mother wouldn't want you to be worrying about her," Father says. "That's thinking backward. Your mother would want you thinking where you are, and not too far ahead."

THE RED SQUIRRELS WAKE US, running across our roof and up and down the walls outside. They scrabble down under the floor and Father stamps so they get quiet for a moment and then even louder. We laugh.

Even if it's not the forest park, there are animals all around and I don't mean horses. A bird flies in the open window and Father says an abode without birds is like a meal without seasoning. It just takes a different way of looking to see these animals and sometimes that is listening. In the ceiling over the kitchen a pack rat has his nest. Father lifts me up with his headlamp on my head and I see the bright lids of tin cans and broken pieces of mirrors, all shining things. Mice are even quieter, darting across the floor when you look another way. The mousetraps that Mr. Walters gives us we put under the bed but we don't even pull back the springs. Even bigger traps go outside, underground to intercept moles and gophers in their blindness. Father shows me how he sets them wrong so they're already tripped like the animal somehow escaped.

"Varmints," he says, pulling the empty traps out by their chains and holding them up.

"Empty again?" Mr. Walters says. "Look at these holes in the pasture. They're out here, all right."

"Outsmarted again," Father says.

"Horse's hoof gets caught in a gopher hole," Mr. Walters says with his short arms in the air. He doesn't finish what he's saying. He calls them gophers and prairie dogs and ground squirrels. Things and even people can have different names. All that matters is that someone understands what you're talking about.

Mr. Walters is a friendly person and he is curious about us. Father says he watches us with binoculars. It's true that he likes to check on us where we are working and to ask questions. He can do this since he owns the whole farm and pays Father a wage. On his covered back porch he has a washer and dryer that we can use. He takes a list of groceries to the store and brings them back to us saying that it makes him think he should be a vegetarian once he sees how much his meat costs him.

"I know you are a gardener," Mr. Walters says to me. "I know you used to have a garden."

"Yes," I say. "In the forest park I did."

The packets he hands me read: Kale, Carrots, Beets, Turnips, Cabbage.

Mr. Walters has cleared out a whole area of garden for me. He shows me how to mix in the manure to make the dirt blacker. He stands leaning against the fence watching me as I plant the seeds and read the packets.

"Those are autumn vegetables," he says. "By the time they come up you'll be in school."

I set the worms carefully aside. I break up the clods with my trowel. Father is not so far away. He is building a corner brace for the fence along the road. Three horses stand near watching him. He stops digging and checks the sky. A truck drives past and he turns his face away.

"This life here must seem pretty easy for you, Caroline," Mr. Walters says. "I hope it's not boring for you."

"It's a girl's own fault if she's bored," I say. I pull my hand flat along the side of the little trench I dug and collapse the dirt down to bury the seeds. "These vegetables," I say, "are you going to take them or are they for Father and me?"

"I hadn't thought of that," Mr. Walters says. "I guess I figured they'd be yours, that you could share them if you want."

"We'll see," I say.

"Did you ever want to ride a horse?" he says.

"I don't know," I say. "I don't think so. These turnips are all planted."

"I have so many questions about how you were living," Mr. Walters says. "It's remarkable, but your father doesn't seem to want to talk about it. They only tell so much in the newspaper."

"I have a question for you," I say.

"Shoot," he says.

"How come you're all alone?"

"I just am I guess," he says.

"How come you don't have any dogs?" I say.

"Maybe if this was a sheep ranch," he says. "But horses and dogs, they don't always mix."

"I've never seen a person wear both suspenders and a belt," I say.

Mr. Walters laughs. "I believe it," he says. "Well, it works for me."

SOMETIMES WHEN YOU'RE sleeping someone presses on your chest or the flat of your back with their hand and when you wake up no one is there but you can tell in the dark air in the room that someone has been talking to you.

THIS AFTERNOON MR. WALTERS takes Father to pick up a piece of equipment. There's some things he can't lift by himself that Father probably can. Father asks and I say I'll go but Mr. Walters says I'll just be in the way and I say no but he says it'll be dangerous and also boring.

"That's all right, Caroline," Father says. "He's the boss. You just do some reading and some gardening. Don't leave the property. We'll be back by dinner."

I weed one side of the garden and then I stop and listen and there's nothing. Far away in the sky a plane slides along. I put my trowel and gloves away and drink from the hose, then walk out past the horse barn following the barbed wire that stretches all the way to the end of the farm. There's a path worn down along the inside edge where the horses walk around and around. There's a place where the stream hooks back around and I leap across there. If someone sees me, I'll say I am checking the fence to see if it needs any mending.

The sun is hot on top of my head. I should have worn a hat. I go through a gate and the grass is longer here where the horses haven't been at it. The ground is marshier and the reeds are higher than my head so I have to push them away with my hands to keep going. I hear the boys' voices before I see them.

"Chainsaw!" they are yelling, and then a dog barks like it's being strangled.

I have moved closer, right to the edge of the road without hardly noticing. The house is beaten-up yellow with cardboard over one front window and all the rain gutter broken and dangling and a metal ladder leaning there. The dog is a huge black and tan shepherd dog tied to a chain. Chainsaw. The boys are throwing a rolled up newspaper back and forth over the dog's head and it's jerking from one to the other growling and barking trying to get at them. More newspapers are all around the yard like no one ever picks them up and opens them and reads them.

"A girl!" the taller boy yells. The newspaper hits the ground and they're walking at me.

Both their hair is white blond and thin. Their faces are sunburned. The little boy is thinner and his T-shirt is dirtier. The older boy is as tall as I am.

"What kind of girl are you?" he says.

"What kind of boy are you?" I say.

"Are you a tomboy?" he says.

"I'm a girl," I say.

"What are you doing on our property?"

"I'm not," I say. "I'm on the road."

"Who said you can watch us?" he says.

"Does your dog bite?" I say.

"Chainsaw?" he says and looks back. "I don't know. She might."

"Chainsaw's deaf," the smaller boy says. "She's old, that motherfucker."

"You can't call a girl dog a motherfucker," the other boy says.

"Yes you can."

"I'm Caroline," I say. "Can I play with you?"

These brothers, the older one is named Ben and the little one is Michael and the game we play is where Michael tries to spray us with the hose and then he has a gun with rubber darts and we run around the house screaming with Chainsaw barking and trying to reach us and I can't tell if she's playing. Then Michael's got a slingshot called a wrist rocket and we're climbing up the ladder onto the roof. The shingles are slippery with grit. The hose sprays up that far and gets Ben in the face.

"Asshole!" he says.

It's fun. We're holding on to the chimney and Michael is still on the ground. A chunk of gravel hits me in the leg and it stings.

"Bitch!" I say.

Michael calls up at us. "Let's switch around," he says.

"Only if you can get Chainsaw up here," Ben says.

The dog has her front paws on the ladder and it's sliding like it might fall down. I wonder if we'd be trapped, if Michael would be strong enough to set the ladder back up or if he'd just rather leave us up here. We start throwing down sticks and laughing and shouting when a horn honks and a dented up blue station wagon with plastic wood on only one side skids into the driveway.

The lady who climbs up has wild blond hair and a flowered blouse and jeans on. She holds a brown paper bag against her.

"Boys!" she says. "What did we agree about the roof? You want the police to come again?"

We're halfway down the ladder before she notices me.

"I wish I could blame you for their behavior," she says. "Chainsaw! Back off."

The dog is sniffing at the bag of groceries.

Inside she gives us a glass of milk with strawberry powder which is sweet and good.

"My name's Caroline," I say. "I live right over there."

"I know who you are," she says. "You're the hillbilly girl that lived in the park."

"I'm a regular girl," I say.

"You look like a regular girl," she says, "but I heard about you on the radio, how you slept inside a cave for four years, all the things you did."

The cupboards are all open and she's sliding in one can after another.

"Crazy," she says. "What grade will you be in?"

"Eighth," I say.

"Same school as Ben," she says. "He probably won't talk to you at school, but you shouldn't feel bad about that."

"I won't," I say. "I might not even talk to him."

The two glasses next to me are empty with pink sludge at the bottom. The boys have already gone back outside.

I DREAM OF RUNNING BAREFOOT in the forest park where I can feel the leaves slapping around me and no one can keep up or catch me and I kick through the snarls of ivy and kick Father beneath the sheets. Or I kick and wake myself with my foot out over the air next to the bed since he's not in the bed. Father has his own helicopter dreams and now he's seeing them in the day too and when I wake up at night usually his eyes are open or he's standing at the window or he's not in the room at all.

I walk into the hallway and through the bathroom, into my empty room. We make up the bed in Father's room but here we mess up the blankets and leave them that way so it looks like I sleep in my bed even though I have never slept there. Randy glows atop the dresser and I pick him up and whisper my secrets into the hole of his stomach, holding my thumb over the hole in his anus so they won't slip out until they settle.

"I played with boys," I say quietly. "Maybe they will be my friends."

In the front room Father is sitting at the table with the light on and writing in his notebook.

"Did you sleep?" I say.

"Do I look like I need my beauty sleep, Caroline? You better comb your hair now, so they don't see you with that birdnest on your head."

Out the window it's dawn. Father's pointing at the sky like a helicopter might be out there watching but there's nothing I can see in the gray clouds.

"I am trying so hard to figure all these things out," he says. "I want you to know that. I don't want you to think I'm not doing anything about it. There is no place on this farm where we can't be seen except for in this house but then they can watch it and see us come and go so they know when we're in here."

"They can't be watching us all the time," I say.

"In the war they dug tunnels," Father says. "Straight down under the floorboards and then underground, coming up into the air far away where no one was looking."

"That's a long tunnel," I say.

Out the window the horses are biting at each other and shifting around waiting for the sun. They watch me when I practice my running but they don't race along the fence like sometimes they do with cars.

A horse can walk and trot and canter and gallop. These are what are known as gaits.

WE ARE UP IRRIGATING when we see the yellow truck coming. It turns in at the farm and instead of turning toward the big house it drives to ours where it stops. The muddy water slips straight around Father's wrists with his hands hidden underwater holding stones to weigh down the plastic dam. I am helping with a slippery piece of sod up on the high bank.

"Those people are taking things out of that truck," I say.

"I guess we better check on what they're doing," he says.

With the wet muddy shovel over his shoulder he leads the way down the slope through the tall grass. I walk in the trail he makes and the grass makes dry slippery sounds around his legs. Next to us the water spills down the slope. It has only reached halfway down seeping in before it slides further, not as fast as us and then it's dry on both sides of us and we're closer, it's easier to see our house. It's hard to walk fast in these black rubber boots.

The yellow truck says RYDER on the side. The man in the open back I have never seen before. He holds a box and wears a baseball cap and blue coveralls.

"Hello," he says.

"This is some kind of misunderstanding," Father says, and then Miss Jean Bauer comes around the side of the truck.

"Caroline!" she says. "You look great. A little muddy, but great."

She looks different without her white coat and in her red boots. Not as old. Her voice is the same. The gray stripe in her hair swoops back.

"It's you," Father says.

"We didn't want to go inside," she says. "But we have all these things for you. Come see. The boxes are some new pots and pans, more clothes. These are all things people sent in, things they wanted to give you when they read about you in the newspaper or heard about you on the radio."

"We don't need any more things," Father says. "Do we have to accept them?"

The first thing I see around the other side is the bicycles shining in the sun. The big one is blue and the smaller one is yellow.

"Go ahead," Miss Jean Bauer says. "You can ride it."

"I don't know how," I say.

"You've never ridden a bike?"

"No."

"Your father will teach you," she says.

"You will?" I say.

Father is stabbing at the ground with the sharp blade of the shovel. He doesn't say anything at first but then leans the shovel against the fence and walks over to the blue bicycle.

"All right," he says. "A little later. I just never had a bicycle with so many gears on it. That's what they are, right?" He smiles halfway like he's made a decision and then picks up a box and carries it into the house.

"Have you been reading the books I gave you for school?" Miss Jean Bauer says.

"Yes," I say.

"Are you happy these days?" she says.

"Yes," I say. "Are you?"

"Mostly," she says. "I'm happy to see you doing so well, Caroline. Adjusting. Wait, look here at these." She bends back the flaps of a box and inside I see gold. The books inside are packed tight. "Encyclopedias. Every single letter," Miss Jean Bauer says.

"But these are World Book," I say. "Mine were Britannica."

"They'll be fine," Father says, passing behind me with another box. "We'll figure it out. Say thank you."

"Thank you," I say.

From the front of the truck Miss Jean Bauer brings a paper bag that holds the things she herself has brought for me. The first thing I can tell the shape of it through the bag. It's Randy's stand with the shining metal piece that fits the hole in his stomach so he doesn't have to lie on his side.

"On that cassette tape," she says, "is a recording of the stories you told me when I showed you the pictures. Those were excellent stories. Sometime you might want to listen to them."

"Thank you," I say holding the bag against me. I have no radio or machine that will play a cassette tape but I don't tell her this.

Next to the bicycle Father squints. He kicks at the kickstand then sits on the seat. When he stands and pumps the pedals he whoops. He swerves out through the grass and all the horses startle away from the fence not sure what he is.

TODAY A LADY RIDING a tall chestnut horse comes along close to me. Her hair is in a straight blond braid against her black vest. My black hair is in a ponytail which does not really look like the horse's tail.

"Hi," the lady says. Sitting on her horse, she is taller than I am where I stand on the fence. The horse turns a little, its head. Its eye is brown. It shifts its metal bit in its mouth under its tongue. Its nose and nostril look very soft.

"Hello," I say.

"Do you ride?" she says.

"No," I say. "I have a bicycle that I'm learning on, though."

"What's your name?"

"Caroline," I say. "What's your horse's name?"

"Boomer."

"Boomer," I say.

"Are you someone's girl?"

"Yes," I say.

I do not stay to watch her take off the saddle and brush her horse down. Instead I go into our house to study. I read one of the schoolbooks about the American presidents who I already knew about from Father teaching me in the forest park. These days he doesn't teach me but only says to read the encyclopedias and then for school to do whatever Miss Jean Bauer said to do.

In the L encyclopedia I am reading about lions who are large carnivores and live in Africa. They reach nine feet long and four hundred pounds and prey on zebras and antelopes. Their groups are known as prides. Below that I read about lipreading which is a way for deaf people to recognize words by the way you move your mouth. It was discovered after a war where there were deafened soldiers. This is so much better than before when I had only the dictionary when the definitions were so short and turned back on each other. Here's some of my writing from back then:

A chain saw is a portable power saw linked to an end-less chain. Endless means boundless, an endless universe, an endless conversation. Continuous. An endless chain. A conversation is a spoken exchange of thoughts, opinions and feelings. A feeling is a tender emotion. An emotion is a state of mental agitation or disturbance, a feeling.

Father comes in the door and hangs his straw hat on a hook and his hair is sweaty and crushed down.

"Studying," he says. "Good."

"What if," I say, "people at school have heard about me before, like in the newspaper or something?"

"Well," he says, "that's part of it. They say you're going to have an ordinary childhood, but that's not so easy." He reaches out and touches my shoulder, then the edge of my ear. He says, "It's not so easy because you're not ordinary. Regular won't fit you."

"But what if the kids make fun of me?" I say.

"You're bigger than that," he says. "You won't even hear it. You've been in a classroom before, after all."

"Yes, but I can hardly remember that," I say. "You told me to forget that."

"Are there leftovers from last night?" he says. "That rice?"

"Yes," I say. I turn toward him but I do not make any noise when I say that yes.

"What?" he says.

"I was trying to see if you can read lips," I say. "I watched the ladies riding today. They were beautiful. Do you think I'll ever ride a horse?"

"Those aren't even real people," Father says. "And half of them are sent out here just to spy on us."

"Do you think Miss Jean Bauer is pretty?" I say.

Father unlaces his boots and long strands of grass fall out. His whiskers have a gray part under his mouth that is new. He leaves his boots by the door with the right one standing and the left one tipped over.

"I really have to take a shower," he says. "Did you say if there was any rice left?"

"I thought the rotors of helicopters made such a racket," I say. "I've never heard anything."

"They can make quieter ones now," he says. "If they can make a plane that takes off straight up they can certainly make a silent helicopter, Caroline. They can see at night, too, and even the heat of your body."

"What does that look like?" I say. "Do they see the horses, too?"

"The horses' heat is a different color," he says.

I STAND ON THE COVERED back porch of Mr. Walters taking the straight pins and the stiff cardboard bodies out of the school clothes that Miss Jean Bauer brought me. There are still clothes in my dresser that I have never worn but I want to wash them so they'll be soft and not have creases when I first wear them to school. I think some days that I will like it there and that it's good that I'll have the same clothes as everyone.

Mr. Walters comes out the screen door and opens the metal refrigerator he keeps there. He takes out a tall silver can of beer and snaps the top and takes a drink.

"One day I'll come out here and you'll be taller than I am," he says.

"If I keep growing," I say. "I don't think I've stopped yet."

"I doubt it," he says. "How's your garden coming?"

"Good."

"Doing some laundry?" he says. "Different than doing it at your special place in the stream, I bet."

"We used the Laundromat sometimes," I say. "These are all school clothes. I'm just getting ready."

"That'll be interesting," he says, "once you spend some more time with kids your age instead of working around with your father all the time. I wonder how much that will change you, how you act."

"I act like a girl," I say. I stab the pins into the cardboard bodies so they will not get lost.

"I'm not saying anything like that," Mr. Walters says.

I put in the detergent and the clothes and I turn and walk back outside into the sun which blinds me for a moment. I sneeze. Once in a hard rain we soaped up our clothes in the forest park and hung them up to rinse from the branches. From a ways away it looked like ten headless people flying through the trees.

IN THE METHODIST CHURCH there is a choir wearing purple robes up at the front and the minister wears a white robe. He is not just someone's father taking a turn like in the church when I was a little girl. In that church people stood up in the crowd and said why they knew the church was true but here we just repeat words in our programs and the hymns in the hymnbook are not the ones I know. We stand to sing. We keep standing up and sitting down.

Father can carry a tune. I can hear his voice past mine and separate from all the others. Deeper. He holds the heavy red hymnal open with one hand and his other on my shoulder. When we sit down a couple girls look back at us and I wonder if they'll be at my school but I cannot tell if the people around us know who we are. I do not see Ben or Michael or their mother or anyone we know. The gold plate comes down our row and Father hands me a five-dollar bill to put inside.

Afterwards on the way out he is all smiling and shaking hands. People say I look pretty in my yellow dress. Really I only want to get outside into the sun and air, away from the crowd and candles and the dusty curtains. I don't want to sing for another week.

The best part of church is the big hill. On the way we have to ride up it and halfway to the top I get off and push. Father's bicycle wags back and forth with him standing on the pedals and at the top he shouts and waits for me. It's on the way home that the big hill is the best. Then I pedal hard and bend low. I scream and coast and the wind blows the braids out of my hair and my yellow dress around my waist I'm going so fast. Father roars behind me and he's never beaten me to the bottom.

Later we have changed out of our church clothes and I make sandwiches. Father's bracelets slide along his forearm as he writes in his small notebook. He has cut a piece of cardboard to cover the window next to where he likes to sit so no one can see him.

"Are you growing a beard?" I say. "It looks like you stopped shaving your face."

"What do you really think about that church?" he says. "Do you believe any of that?"

"It's different than the one I remember," I say, "when I was little."

"Is that what I asked you?" he says.

"No," I say. "I like the bicycle riding part."

"Good, Caroline," he says.

"Why?" I say. "Do you believe that?"

"I believe that's a good looking sandwich," he says. "Well, church. No matter how ridiculous it is sometimes some worthwhile things get said."

"So that's why we go?" I say.

"Appearances count," Father says. "When they see us riding our bikes to church, when they hear us sing and we dress up on Sunday that makes them believe certain things about us."

"Like what?" I say.

"That we're like them," he says. "That we believe the same things. That makes them happy, to see us doing what they're doing."

THE HORSES IN THE MOONLIGHT bite and kick at each other with their sharp metal hooves.

WHEN FATHER CUTS the hay field he pulls the swather behind the tractor and it takes down the tall grass leaving a line like he's erasing the field a stripe at a time or like a haircut. It's pretty and it's sad to watch, the color green goes darker where it's cut and I watch from the branches of an aspen I climb. Every time he turns the corner he waves to me. If he hits a rock or there's some snag or tangle or jam he stops and climbs down to fix it.

Today he wears a blue and white striped engineer's cap. He changes hats almost every day so anyone watching might not know it's him. He's given me four bandanas to wear on different days on my head: red, blue, yellow, camouflage.

The engine quiets down and for a while he's sitting with his back against the tractor's tall wheel without moving or getting up to fix anything so I climb down from the aspen and hop across the stream and walk down the slope of stubble and long cut grass careful not to kick it out of its straight rows. I leap sideways at a black snake but see then that it's cut in two, in three, the edges red from the sharp blades of the swather.

Father doesn't see me coming, he's not looking for me, the sound of the tractor idling covers my footsteps. His hat is off and his face is darker down low, a necklace of white around his neck when he takes his shirt off at night. He doesn't look up until he feels my shadow.

"Are you crying?" I say.

"No," he says. "Not really. It's just my eyes, Caroline."

The tractor is not broken. He's just taking a break. Then he lets me sit on his lap even though Mr. Walters does not like me on the tractor and the engine is so loud it's impossible to talk. I steer the tractor as we cut down the tall grass. You have to look straight ahead where you're going and at the same time out of the side of your eye watch the big black wheel turning just behind you on the right since you want it rolling just on the line of what's been cut so the swather behind you doesn't miss one stalk.

THE DAYS ARE STILL long even though they're getting shorter. The sun slants across the field. The big round yellow bales are spaced all the way across from fence to fence and all the way up the slope to the stream.

"Are you counting them?" I say to Father who is standing at the window looking out. "How many are there?" I say.

"You see those shadows?" he says. "Down next to every bale? A person could easily hide in every one of those black shadows."

"Could be," I say. I don't say that we could go out and check, that I doubt it.

"Here," he says, holding out my backpack that I haven't seen in a long time. "We're going on a trip. Pack up some things."

"We're going now?" I say. "Where?"

"Once it's dark," he says.

"This is our house," I say. "Are we coming back?"

"We'll see," he says.

"How long?" I say.

"Four days, maybe? Just put whatever you can in your pack. Some clothes."

I go into my room and pull out the dresser drawers. I have so many clothes. While I'm deciding, Father comes in and watches me.

"Don't take those new school clothes," he says. "Those will draw attention. They'll recognize you. That's why they gave them to you. So they can keep track."

"Do you want to pack for me?" I say.

"No," he says. "I don't. But here, here's something I want you to keep."

It's a plastic card that fits in the Wells Fargo ATM machine, just like his card. I am not to use it unless Father says or unless something happens to him. I memorize the number I need to memorize by looking at the spots on Randy's body. One half-way down his throat, one on his hoof. I put him in my pack, and then my forest pants that I haven't worn for a long time and probably don't even fit me anymore. I put the Wells Fargo card in the front pocket of my pack with my library card that I've almost forgotten about.

Once it's dark we go out the back door, close around our house.

"It would be faster to ride," I say as we pass the bicycles where they are leaned against the wall, under the roof's overhang.

"No," Father says. "We leave those here."

We hurry without talking past the barn, along the fence. The horses follow on the other side. Father hisses but they keep coming lined up in single file under the moon like they are saying good-bye or trying to give us away by drawing attention. They do not give us away.

I look back once at our house with all our things in it. In the big house yellow lights shine in the square windows but nothing moves.

"How far are we walking?" I finally say, out on the road where we can't see the houses anymore.

"Not far," Father says. "Only to a bus stop. You remember a long time ago, that special way we rode the bus?"

"Yes," I say.

Four

THE HEADLIGHTS GROW WIDER and I stand alone at the stop. I climb on and pay my fare and just then Father comes running up slapping the side of the bus like he almost missed it and like we aren't together. He sits in the back of the bus and I sit in the middle, on the right side.

Outside the sky is darker than the clouds and inside the bus the lights flicker on and off. I see my face in the window's reflection, then the dark fields, then my face again. On my head I wear a stocking cap with all my hair pushed up inside it so maybe I look like a boy. I close my eyes to rest since Father told me at the bus stop that it might be a long night. I open my eyes and we come down through the curving streets, into the lights. I recognize some of the buildings' shapes and the names of the streets: Salmon, Jefferson, Oak.

Father walks to the front to get off and I go out the back door. We're downtown in the city of Portland and I'm excited and afraid and a little disappointed. We might sleep in a doorway or down along the river which we have done before a long time ago.

"What?" I say to Father, whispering without really facing him.

"Did you hold on to your transfer?" he says. "Good girl. Now we catch one more bus. Here goes."

We're not even downtown for ten minutes and we don't talk

to anyone. We climb onto the next bus, careful that others get on between us so it looks like we are not together.

We're out again in fifteen minutes, past dark houses and parked cars. A dog barks. Father and I walk on opposite sides of the street, walking at the same speed. The rain barely starts and we are across the mowed park then on the little trail along Balch Creek, safe under the trees.

An owl calls hollow from one side then the other. We're not talking. We turn right at the stone house and it is harder to walk and find our way than I remember, like the trees have grown up in new places while we were gone and thickened the dark. I feel like I'm back where I belong and then something else sharp I'm not sure what.

Father is careful. His headlamp is around his head but he doesn't switch it on until we're close. Our feet find the old steppingstones.

The circle of light darts and settles. I am glad I can't see all this at once even if every sad thing adds up the way I see it so later I will remember them lit up and lost. Part of the roof has been torn off our old house so the plastic and tarps show. There's a hole where maybe someone's foot went through and I think how that would be, to be reading a book or playing chess or lying in bed when a foot comes punching through the ceiling.

There's a fire ring in the middle of our clearing, all wet and charred logs with blackened beer cans crushed up. Keystone is the name of the brand of beer. There's cigarette butts and shreds of plastic bags.

"Oh man, oh man," Father says. His hands are on his head and he's turning slow circles so the beam of light flashes against the tree trunks, up into the branches, there and gone, resting on a white sign that says SHERIFF but Father can read it faster than I can and the light flashes away, down into our house which is empty.

"Of course, of course of course this is how it is," Father says. "This is exactly the kind of thing they love to do, every single time. Oh man, Caroline."

Our green Coleman stove and our kettle and our pots and pans and everything is gone just like I said they would be taken. The only thing left really is my encyclopedias and they're all damp and pulled off the shelf and piled on the floor. There's black mold growing in the pages so they're thicker than they should be with the spines stretched open. I pick up the L and try but it smells bad and the pages are stuck together so I drop it.

"Do we have to sleep here?" I say.

"We could," Father says, "but I don't think I can."

Instead we sleep in the hollow beneath a fallen tree trunk. Father spreads a blue tarp beneath us, on top of ferns and moss. He's brought a blanket from our house on the farm to put over us. We're in all our clothes, holding hands. The trees scratch and creak.

"At least we're back," I say.

"Now, Caroline," Father says. "Try to sleep."

I turn over and over again. I listen. I am not asleep since I want to see it all again in the morning and since I am a little afraid and since I can tell that Father is also not asleep.

THERE IS FROST ON the blanket in the morning, just barely. My ear that is outside of the blanket is cold. Father is already up slapping his legs and stretching his arms over his head trying to get warm.

"This is great," he says. "Just like old times." He keeps saying things like this and the more he says the less true it sounds.

"Caroline!" he says. He's pulling plastic bags out of his pack. "Breakfast," he says.

He's brought peanut butter and jelly sandwiches and while we eat them I think of our refrigerator and the full jar of jelly there and the orange juice, and the toaster on the counter.

"What do you want to do today?" he says.

"I don't know," I say. "Start building a new house, I guess."

"Let's walk around a little," he says. "Stay warm until the sun comes up."

We walk on paths and not on paths. Wet ferns stripe our legs. The sky is overcast and there's nothing to say. It's like every animal is hibernating or hiding. Father isn't even bothering to make a trail. He kicks sticks out of the way, cracks them. He tears leaves with his hands. And then he sees something and crashes sideways though the bushes. He stretches to reach up into the crook of a tree. Into a hollow.

His hand comes out with his special oilskin holder, folded and rolled up and tied tight. It is easy to find or make do to replace almost anything except a good knife or scissors and he has found his knives and his long scissors where they'd been hidden.

He hands me my red pocketknife and I cut my fingernails with the tiny scissors and scatter them around. Next I cut his beard with these, careful around his mouth. He pulls the skin tight and I snip along, just the long ones that stick out. He is sitting on a stump and next I stand straight.

"How would it be if we cut it all off this time?" he says. "If I cut it as short as mine?"

"Why?" I say.

"So you'll look different."

"The same," I say. "I don't want to look like anyone else."

Father cuts my black hair straight across my back at the bottom of the shoulder blades so I'll still be able to pull it back in a rubber band or he can French braid it. His hair is harder to cut. It is brown and gray and curls and he says he doesn't care how it looks because he'll be wearing a lot of hats during the winter. I take hold of his hair and cut it close, as thick as my finger, right above where I'm holding.

At the end he takes off his jacket and flaps it all around and we run laughing from all the loose hairs floating through the air like we always used to.

The sun has actually come out. We're laughing. Father runs ahead slapping his head, the last hairs falling down behind him and I'm chasing. He's ahead and when I catch up he's not laughing anymore. He's standing still. I can't tell what's happened and what's changed.

"Listen," he says. "I was thinking it might be good for us to have some alone time just to range around and remember. So we can get comfortable again."

"Are you going to stay in the forest park?" I say. "I can come with you."

"Let's just decide on our watches," he says, "and then we'll meet back where we slept. You can find that again, right?

Father does not check back. He disappears through the trees tall and uncertain, not in any kind of straight line. The maple leaves are bright red and yellow and orange against the green pines. After a while that is all I can see.

First I take off my shoes and socks then put them back on since the ground is cold and wet and hard. I run a little ways and then stop so I can think. No one can see me, I'm thinking. I'm thinking how Father says someone could always see us on the farm but now here in the forest park I'm not even sure no one is watching. With my short fingernail I scratch Hello in the green of a leaf.

I circle back to get Randy, just in case. His body is cold, stiffer than usual. When I take him out of my pack I put him back in and put the whole thing on my back since I just don't know.

I walk out along the edge of the forest park and there are no criminals in their orange outfits. I do not see or hear any dogs.

"What?" I yell in the loudest voice I have ever used in the forest park. "Lala!" I say. Nothing happens and no one answers except the birds are quiet for a moment before they start up talking again.

FATHER IS ALREADY WAITING when I come back and I am early. He stands up and swings his frame pack onto his back.

"We need to find the men's camp," he says.

"I thought we decided never to go back," I say.

"Caroline," he says. "So much has changed. Stay close to me."

We walk the old path that is not a real path but when we get to the men's camp it is abandoned. It is more overgrown even than our old house was. Someone probably the rangers has picked up the trash and other than the fire rings and broken glass and torn off tree branches a person might not even know.

It's easy enough even for me to see the direction the men went. How they dragged things and stepped all over the ferns and the little maples. Father and I follow all this for only another ten minutes and then I hear a voice call out low saying how we look and then another lookout who knows who we are calls out our names.

There's only one fire. Dirty wool blankets and stained, soggy sleeping bags hang from branches. There's only about twenty people. None of the Skeleton Family, no Nameless of course but I can't even see Richard and if he was here he would at least come talk to me, or try to talk to me. It's like every person has been replaced by another person even if they all look the same and wear the kind of clothes. If Richard was here I see that I would be kind of happy but he is not.

It is only Clarence coming over to talk to us. His red beard is longer and he wears a wool-blanket poncho and a bright orange hunter's cap that anyone could see a mile away. Instead of shoes he's got the inside felt liners from snowmobile boots and they're filthy and shredded up. Closer to us I can see he's frowning.

"What?" he says. "You know better. This is ridiculous."

"Hold on, now," Father says, and his deep voice slows Clarence. "I thought you might have some of our things, that were left behind when we went away."

"Since you went away!" Clarence says. "That's an excellent way to put it. Since you've been away. Well, since you've been away what you've done is rain down shit on everybody and brought cops through here like they never even cared before. You and your daughter! Do you even know? I can't believe you would come back here and lead them to us again not to mention that this is the exact first place they'll come looking for you. Stupid."

I wait for Father to say something and so does Clarence. I look up and I can't even see where the lookouts are, the men who called our approach. I think how last night I didn't even check the lookout over our old house, how someone could have been up there listening and waiting. But Father doesn't say anything right away and Clarence just kicks his legs back around and goes back to the fire and sits down and doesn't look back.

Over to the left then I see the shredded paper people. There's matchbooks all around on the ground and the silver plastic from sheets of pills. They're cooking something on our green Coleman stove.

"Look," I say. "Look."

"Come on, Caroline," Father says, turning me away. "That's poisoned now."

We cut across a slope, a different direction than the way we came. I feel that I might not know my way.

"Nature ever flows," Father says, "never stands still."

"They might come looking for us, here," I say, "but they'll never find us again. We'll make a new house. We know how."

"He's right it was stupid," Father says. "Even for one night. They won't find us here because it was never the plan to stay here. We only came back to get our things, what we could."

"What is the plan?" I say. "Where will we sleep?"

"The main thing is we found our knives," he says, the oilskin holder in his hand.

Father tightens the straps on his pack and we keep walking. A little while later we push through a stand of bushes, into a clearing and I stop since it seems like I've been here before.

"What?" he says.

"Isn't this the place," I say, "where the deer died?"

"What?" he says again.

"Where the dead deer was?" I say.

We start kicking the long grass with our shoes, then pull at it with our hands but don't find a single bone or tooth or even a tuft of hair. Either every last scrap has been taken or this is not the same place at all.

THESE ARE THE WORST DAYS. The rules and the way things work in the city are different, sharper and dirtier than in the forest park but you can still be aware and stay out in the open enough not to get trapped and still not draw attention so people won't want to know who you are and what you're doing, a girl out alone in the city. If someone thinks they know me I am to tell them there's been a misunderstanding, that my name is Elaine and I live in Lake Oswego. If I see a police car or a policeman I am not to run away. I turn my face in another direction. I can look like I am on my way to school or catching the bus home or like I'm shopping for birthday presents or meeting my friends.

There is alone time in the city but that means really that we are apart from each other not that we are alone since there are people everywhere. Mostly they are not looking at you. They think you're looking at them.

I can only sleep decently in the forest park but Father says that's too dangerous, especially to stay in one place and maybe once every two weeks he'll let us sleep in some different part of the forest park but more often we just nap during the day and wander at night. Sometimes it's different parks, even across the river on Mount Tabor or Laurelhurst but there's always homeless people in that park. We've slept in a parking garage in unlocked cars and in the entryway under the metal mailboxes in an apartment building. When you're tired it makes everything in the day harder.

MY HEAD IS BENT OVER the sink in the Fred Meyer bathroom and it doesn't take long. It burns in my nose and throat. Someone knocks on the door and Father tells them to wait. The water is running and running and my back is sore and when I look up all my hair is bleached out to a yellow that doesn't look real. My eyes look different and the edges of my face are harder to see. Father smiles behind me, his beard makes a scratching noise against the collar of his jacket. I look fake and wet. I don't like it at all but would I like it better if my hair stayed black and we were caught and locked up again?

AT PIONEER COURTHOUSE SQUARE there's punk rock kids playing hackysack and smoking cigarettes. The MAX train slides in and out. The food trailers here have stainless steel sides printed in triangles that cut up your reflected face. I order the largest vegetarian burrito, the size is called Honkin.

Sitting on the red brick steps I can't even eat half of it but then I leave it on the bricks and walk away. Father walks over from where he's standing by the Starbucks. This is how we do it, how we share so we're not seen together. If we tried it the other way with him eating first it would draw attention and someone might worry about a girl eating leftover food. We have to think all the time. The two of us together draw a kind of attention since they will look for us to be together.

When he finishes the burrito Father throws the wrapper into a trash can and walks away. I follow. Sometimes I'm across the street, sometimes on the same side trailing behind. If it's raining we have umbrellas and there are signals we have with opening or closing or twirling them but today it is not raining.

I think I know where he's going. My pack slaps my back, Randy's hard nose against my neck. We do all this and yet I'm the small one who people don't see and Father draws attention right away with his strong way of walking and his red frame pack that we have nowhere safe to keep so he carries it everywhere. And still he jerks his head to check behind him and he's drawing attention by trying not to.

I cross the opening of a parking garage, a car coming out and then a wide doorway. I shiver since it seems like maybe the building where we were locked up when we were caught. I walk faster and turn my face away as a police car drives past and turns under the building.

Father says the helicopters over the city are mostly for traffic, to tell people through their radios where there are a lot of cars but there are other people in the helicopters too who are looking down with binoculars for people like us. This is one reason Father wears the piece of mirror taped to the top of his engineer's cap, so it reflects back up whoever's face is trying to look down at him. As he walks the sun reflects in the mirror and slides shining lights all along the brick wall above his head. If he bends down to tie his shoes it can hit you sharp in the eyes.

I was right: He goes into the Mailboxes store. When we lived on the farm Father switched our address to a close post office and before we left the farm he rode his bicycle to town and switched it to this place. Smart. Only he is nervous when he comes out with the envelope in his hand so I can see that he got it, that everything's fine. Next, the Wells Fargo machine, to deposit the check.

He's ten feet in front of me on the same side of the street when a black man in a baseball cap comes out of a door and reaches out to touch Father's arm.

"Jerry!" he says to Father. "Haven't seen you in a long, long time. Missing a lot of meetings, my man. You staying healthy?"

"Been out of town," Father says like he's trying to get past.

"I keep getting caught up on the fourth step," the man says. "Moral inventory, you know. You coming back?"

"At present I am a sojourner in civilized life again," Father says. "I better get on my way."

"Way you talk," the man says. "Cracks my shit up."

We keep walking. I talk to Father's back and he does not turn around so if you saw us you'd think we were talking to ourselves and not having a conversation.

"Your name's not Jerry," I say.

"That's just what he knows me by," he says.

"Why?" I say. "How does he know you?"

Two more police cars drive by. I look at three mannequins wearing dresses in a shop window so the space between Father and me can grow wider. Then I catch up.

"How does he know you?" I say.

"Hardly," Father says. "I liked that burrito."

"And what's a sojourner?" I say.

"Look it up," he says.

He says this when he knows I don't have my dictionary with

me and I'd have to go to the library to look up the word sojourner. The downtown library is very big and homeless people
gather there both inside and outside so we are not allowed to go
there. It's no place to be seen. I've hardly done any homework
or read a thing since we left the farm. Father sometimes writes
in his notebook but it's more like he's adding up numbers or
checking off lists than writing and I haven't seen him reading his
books like he used to. Reading in public draws attention.

IT'S ALMOST GETTING DARK and I come out of the mall and on
the sidewalk a shepherd dog in a red vest is looking right at me.
I know I'm caught. If I turn or run, it will chase me. I remember
my hair and I try to not walk or move like me. I am already
thinking what Father will do and whether I'll tell about the hotel
and everything else.

The dog's leash is short though and it's held by a lady in
square sunglasses and her brown hair back in a ponytail. She's
not looking at me like the dog is and then I see how the writing
on the red vest does not say POLICE but something else I cannot
read. The dog is kind of pulling this woman along as they walk
away and I see then that it is that the lady is blind. So I am not
caught and I keep walking.

It's darker now, late enough that the workers have left the
hotel. It stands all fenced in. They didn't knock it down today.
The signs on the fence say DEMOLITION and every night I have
to find a new way through. I count the floors up all the steps and
around all the trash in the stairwells, the broken shopping cart
and everything else.

In our room Father has taken everything out of my little pack and put it neatly on the mattress. He is taking things from his pack and putting it in mine. He kisses me but he's thinking of something else.

"I saw a blind lady," I say.

"I think I have to go out," he says. "For a while. I'm waiting to hear from someone."

"I bet I know who," I say.

Father knows plenty of people in the city. He has a lot of different names. I don't have to know these people and it's better if they don't know me. Some of them are from other times and some are helpful now. Vincent is one of these people, Vincent who is even taller than Father but much skinnier and probably weighs half as much. He always wears dark creased slacks and a white shirt. His shoes shine. I am not to talk to him. I am never to be alone with him not that I'd want to be. When he walks he hardly bends his knees.

There's a knock at the door then and Father looks up. Through the peephole I can see Vincent's face: His black beard is pointed and the hair on his head is exactly the same length as that beard so it's like a helmet where you can only see the skin of his face around his mouth and high on his cheeks and his white forehead and black eyes.

"Open the door," Father says. "Let's see what he wants."

Vincent is not winded from walking all those flights of stairs.

"Hello," he says. "I have come. I have come because there's something to do."

Vincent has a different way of talking with his voice hardly rising or falling and there are no commas in anything he says. I count for a full minute and Father's eyes blink eight times and

Vincent's only blink once. My eyes blink nine times in a minute which is hard to test when I'm paying attention. All I'm trying to get clear is that Vincent's eyes hardly blink.

"Does this interest you?" he says.

"Can you maybe give me a little more information?" Father says.

"It's a delivery," Vincent says.

"More wire?" Father says.

"A delivery and a pickup," Vincent says. "And then perhaps another delivery. That's what I know."

"All right," Father says, "same deal as last time. Caroline, you lock the door. I'll be back late, after you're asleep."

They leave the room and I lock the door and after a little while I can see out the window, them getting into Vincent's white Chrysler K-Car with the trunk that opens and closes as it drives away from the hotel which is all surrounded by fences and barbed wire.

There is not glass in all our windows so it's almost as good as sleeping outside, I can breathe halfway decently. We have a mattress that's queen-sized, bigger than we've ever had and than we need. There are only beds from the sixth floor up. Below that the rooms are empty since Father says the workmen probably got tired of emptying it when they're going to knock the whole building down anyway and gravity will do that work for them. He says this was a nice hotel, once, over a hundred years ago. Now there's no electricity and all the water's been turned off. All the toilets are full or there's just trash in them but that's all right since we use a chamber pot again and some of the drains still drain. Father carries buckets of water up all the stairs. It stretches out my arms and hurts my fingers to try. You have to stay away from the elevators even though the doors are closed. It is dangerous.

I do everything I can think of doing in our room. I straighten all my things and I write. I have no books to read and I am not to read Father's books or to look inside his pack. Here I am, a girl in this hotel and no one knows I'm inside here. The building that Miss Jean Bauer works in is not far away and I wonder if she still thinks about me and what she would say if she knew I was this close.

Days, weeks and maybe a month has gone. Mostly we stay here in the hotel at night. Father and I change the hands on our watches around so much that it confuses the numbers in the little window that would tell me the day. It is hard to keep the days straight.

Alone I am not to unlock the door or leave our room at night without Father but I do. I wander with the headlamp in my hand, my fingers around it so the light won't draw attention. I wear shoes because of the nails and dirt and dust. Other people sleep here but they are afraid of Father. He won't let anyone else sleep on the seventh floor or even above us. I do go above us to the eighth floor and even the ninth floor. I don't dare go below the sixth. The door to the rooftop is locked with a thick chain around all the handles.

I wonder about my bedroom that I never slept in, in our house at the farm. I think about all my clothes I never wore and if they're still in my wooden dresser, washed once and folded and waiting. I would wear those to school and by now I would be in school. Kids would maybe have called me names but there also would have been good parts. All the books and games and maybe someone would like me after they got used to me and I was used to everything. I would have had the same clothes as everyone but now they are far away.

Now my clothes are dirty and it's even hard to keep my skin and hair clean. Waiting for Father to come back I take out the buttons and thimbles and green plastic army men and I have a square sheet of cardboard I've lined into a chessboard. I have pennies for pawns and silver batteries for queens, sparkplugs for bishops. Kings and rooks and knights I haven't figured out yet for sure so I use quarters and dimes and nickels. I play against Randy, with him on his side on the mattress and I play both sides really against myself which doesn't work. I try two openings and then stop. I write some of this out and curl up on the mattress.

I WAKE UP WHEN Father comes home since he knocks his knock and I have to unlock the locks.

"Tired," he says, sitting on the mattress, kicking off his boots.

"Your checks are still coming," I say. "We don't need money so much you have to work for Vincent, do we?"

"I'm planning ahead," Father says. "Caroline, you know that. The checks, I'm not certain they'll follow us where we're going."

"Where are we going?"

"Trust me," he says.

"Still," I say. "What are you doing?"

"We can only do our best," Father says. "We can't do better than our best." He falls back and groans.

"That wire with Vincent," I say, "that wasn't stolen?"

"His name is Victor," Father says. "I don't know that I'll work with him again."

"This is not the way we used to be," I say. "This is not a way we were ever supposed to be."

Father sits up and begins to scrabble his hands along the floor until he finds the headlamp. Then he digs through his pack until he finds his notebook. He pages through it.

"The other terror," he says, "the other terror that scares us from self-trust is our consistency. With consistency a great soul has simply nothing to do. He may as well concern himself with his shadow on the wall."

I listen. The shadows on our wall are only the crossed lines of the window frame and the square edge of another building.

"It would be better," I say, "if you talked to me instead of reading at me."

"They're the same thing, really," Father says. With the headlamp his face is so bright I can't see his expression.

"No," I say. "One comes out of you and the other comes out of someone else."

"Think about that, Caroline," he says. "Whether or not that's actually true."

He switches off the headlamp and turns over, then over again pulling the blanket away from me.

"Do you ever think about all our things?" I say. "Back at the farm? Like our bicycles?"

"Those were not really our things," Father says. "You know that."

I don't say anything else. I know we have to sleep so we'll get up in time since during the day all the workmen come with their yellow hardhats. Some night we'll come home and this room where I'm sleeping will be gone. There will only be air here in the sky and the bricks and walls and mattresses and everything will have collapsed into a pile to be taken away. If we're not too far away in the city on the day it happens we might hear it fall.

TO SOJOURN IS TO reside temporarily, so a sojourner is temporarily residing. To reside is to live in a place permanently or for an extended period. To extend is to open or straighten or unbend.

TODAY ON THE ESPLANADE a girl in a hooded sweatshirt and duct-taped shoes skateboards past. Pushing hard and suddenly leaping to scrape the bottom of her board along the next bench and then rolling backward past me, near where my feet are pointed.

"Nice," I say but she doesn't hear me and keeps going and I'm thinking that girl could be my friend. Already she's out of reach out across the walkway under the Steel Bridge and past her, way up the river I can see the pale green towers of the St. Johns Bridge and I look away since I don't want to think of all that back then.

It's stopped raining and the sun is out and there's a couple boats out on the river. I sit on the esplanade closer to the Steel Bridge, between it and the Hawthorne. Down there they're setting up tents for some kind of festival or fair. The fountain over there is on but it's too cold out for the kids to play in it. There's homeless guys drinking, passed out, and a group of street kids with their BMX bikes on the grass. Everyone's smoking cigarettes.

I'd rather be in the forest park but Father says we can't go there anymore. He says we can blend in better in the city. We're meeting at two forty-five and until then he doesn't know where I am and I don't know where he is and I have to be very careful. You have to look like you're going somewhere and if you can you don't ever want to look like you're carrying everything you own. You want to travel light like you have a home and that's where you keep your things. Which we kind of have at the hotel even if I'm surprised at night if even the building is still there.

A girl stands up and trips over one of the bikes and then walks over close to the bench where I'm sitting.

"I thought that was you," she says.

"Thought I was who?" I say.

"Caroline," she says. "Isn't that your name?"

"No," I say.

"That is your name," she says, "or it was, anyway. You changed your hair but I can tell it's you."

This girl's dark hair is all different lengths and the black mascara on her eyelashes is also on her skin around her eyes. She wears a too big down jacket with filthy jeans and rubber sandals with tube socks. A white scar stretches like a tongue up out of her coat, up the side of her neck and around her ear like it must go far down under clothes and hair and be even thicker.

"I don't know who you are," I say.

"It's me," she says. "Taffy. Remember?"

"What happened?" I say. "Where's Valerie?"

I look past her but it's not any members of the Skeleton Family, just street kids I don't know with no adults.

"Your watch is still wrong," she says.

"No," I say. "My watch is right." I've pushed thumbholes in the seams of my black sweater so the arms stay down. Now I pull the cuffs over my watch so she can't see it.

"Something happened," she says. "You didn't hear?"

"No," I say, "but we went away for a while. We're just visiting the city, now."

"It was lightning," she says.

"Are you going to cry?" I say.

"We, the whole family was living under the overpass," she says, "way over there across the river. And we'd got electricity out of a box under there, where Johnny tapped it and got a wire in there so we had a radio and a toaster and an electric blanket. We all had our own orange extension cords."

I look across the river where she's pointing. A man jogs past with a hairy chest and his shirt off. Father is not anywhere close I can see. I'm not to talk to anyone for longer than two minutes.

"They called it a surge," she says. "During the lightning storm we were just sitting there listening to the radio and it came right through the wires and burned everyone."

"I can see," I say.

"Valerie died," she says. "Valerie's dead. We're not ever going to have everyone together again."

"I'm sorry that happened to you," I say.

"I'm staying," she says, "now I'm staying mostly in this guy Jeremy's car. You're still with your father, right?"

"Of course," I say.

"I was thinking," she says. "Could I come with you? I could help out. You'd be glad."

"When we were locked up in the building," I say, "you hardly talked to me."

"That was because of Valerie," she says. "Please."

"It's just the two of us," I say. "Father and me. It's always been like that. We wouldn't know what to do with a third person. I'm sorry about what happened to you. I don't need a little sister right now."

She's gone before she says anything more since Father is here, coming in quiet, sitting on the other end of the bench with a space between us. He talks softly without turning to me.

"Who was that girl?" he says.

"No one," I say.

"She seemed to know you. You seemed to know her. I saw you talking with her for quite some time."

"I met her in the building after we got caught," I say. "She's part of the Skeleton Family."

"Who?" he says.

"She won't talk to me again," I say. "Don't worry."

Father seems to be growing smaller these days even if that cannot be true. The sky looks like it might rain, and after talking to Taffy I am afraid that living in the city like this will make lightning strike us. The mirror taped to Father's cap has pulled the cap sideways so I can see the skin of the side of my face and the dark roots of my hair. He stands then and walks away. I count to thirty and then I follow him.

Five

THE TRAINS ARE A LOT BIGGER up close and even when they move slowly it's not as slow as you think. That's because of their weight. It takes a long distance for them to be able to stop, and sometimes they don't stop but only slow down as they pass through.

We're standing half in the railyard and half out, where the chain-link fence is broken. I look at the city lights and the dark buildings, trying to see the hotel, then the other direction to the dark trees of the forest park.

"Will it be loud inside the train?" I say.

"We'll see," Father says.

"We'll hear," I say.

"Good one, Caroline."

"How can you tell which train is which?" I say.

"The numbers," he says.

"Does it matter which one we catch?" I say. "Where are we going?"

Father doesn't answer. He's wearing black eyeglasses without glass in them. I can't tell if he's trying to slouch or the way he stands has changed. We are trying not to look like ourselves. His red pack is black along the bottom it's so dirty now and there's more duct tape patches and dental floss stitching and the ragged holes where grommets have fallen out. The teeth don't hold on the zipper of my pack so every time I check I have to unzip and zip it again. Randy looks out crushed by all my papers and my underwear and socks. That's all I have that I'm not wearing.

"We're going south," Father says at last. "I don't want you to get any colder than this."

I look up at his face and he's not looking at me. His eyes jerk out along the fence, past the trains, back again.

"What are you looking for?" I say. "Vincent or Victor or whoever?"

"Anyone," he says. "Anyone could be looking for us."

"You're not hiding in a smart way," I say. "All that jerking around draws attention."

Two tracks away a train sits still. It's been here for the last half hour, ever since we came. Now there's a long creak like the train is thinking about moving but nothing happens.

"It's all this light," he says. "It's not dark enough."

"These lamps are on all night," I say. "For the trains."

"Here it comes," Father says. "Stay close to me, don't fall behind. Once I'm on, I'll reach down and pull you up."

"Good," I say.

"Watch your legs, Caroline," he says. "Keep them from getting caught underneath."

We look away from the train as it comes close so the engineer in the front won't see us.

"Now," Father says.

The ground is all black and greasy sharp stones which make it hard to run. The train is sliding by fast enough that the writing is all blurred and we run at an angle aiming for the black square of an open door. But Father slows and circles away then before he even touches the train. I follow him back into the shadows where the fence has come undone.

"What?" I say.

"That wasn't the one," he says.

"Were the numbers wrong?"

"I had a bad feeling," he says. "It was an unlucky train."

"An unlucky train?" I say.

"I think there might have already been people in there," he says. "People we don't want to meet. Hoboes."

"Hoboes?" I say.

We wait some more. I've been imagining us sleeping on a pile of straw all night on the train. Now that I'm closer to the trains, I see that it won't be anything so soft. It's cold and feels colder because of the damp. My skin on my face feels dirty from the trains. My hands are fists inside my mittens. I stamp my feet to feel them.

"Why don't we get on that train that isn't moving?" I say. "Then once it starts up we'll already be on it."

"It could be there for days," Father says. "At least the ones that are already moving we know we won't be sitting here waiting all night."

I know that Father is trying and maybe this all will help. At least we have to get out of the city where he has done so many things I thought he would never do. I tell him this over and over which is one reason I think we're leaving. It's hard to be called a hypocrite by your daughter who you have taught everything. It's hard to stay the same while everything keeps changing around you.

"This is it," Father says, and starts running at an angle to get to the next train.

This time I slip on the sharp black stones so I am further behind. Father reaches the train, he jumps up and takes hold as it slides past and I am trying to get there so he can turn and pull me up but instead he falls off flat on his back, on top of the pack and doesn't move for a moment while the metal wheels clatter by next to his head.

He rolls over finally and crawls back toward the fence, getting his feet under him, his arms dangling.

"Are you all right?" I say. "Haven't you ever done this before?"

"No," Father says. "I'm sorry Caroline. I haven't."

THE BUS STATION is the saddest place to see. Homeless people are asking for spare change outside and I wait out there while Father goes in. When he comes out he turns so no one can see and he has bills of money folded thick in his hand. He gives me some.

"Go in and buy a ticket to Bend," he says. "One way."

"Where?" I say. "I've never heard of that place."

"Bend," he says. "Actually get a round-trip ticket."

"We're coming back?" I say.

"No," he says. "Just buy it that way. Then sit down on the bench in there, once you have the ticket. The bus leaves in half an hour. Same plan as always."

No one inside looks like they're traveling to anywhere they want to go. The clock on the wall says eight fifteen and the bus leaves at eight thirty-five. My watch says eleven twenty-three and so does Father's. He's sitting on another wooden bench reading a newspaper he picked up off the floor.

The bus is more than half empty. I sit alone on the left side in the middle and Father is behind me, six rows back. I am not sad to leave the city of Portland or even the forest park where we don't belong anymore but then I have never heard of Bend and don't know what kind of place it is. No one sits next to me and I bring my feet up sideways on the seat and lean my face against the cold window. Through the broken zipper of my pack I feel Randy's neck and the blue ribbon which is frayed and coming apart even if the knot still holds it tight around him.

We slip away from the buildings, we cross the river and before long we're out on the freeway with dark fields on every side.

Far away is the shape of a long black train. I can't tell who is moving faster and if we were on that train it would be much colder though Father's plan would have succeeded so maybe it would be harder for people to follow where we're going.

IT'S RAINING IN EUGENE. I follow Father when he gets off and I can also tell by reading my ticket that we have to switch to another bus here. It's only five minutes we stand in the station and then we go through all the smokers standing in the doorway and get on the next bus.

The lights inside are off so it's just the shapes of people's heads sitting in the seats and you can't see their faces or if they're looking at you. Father is in the back again and no one sits next to him since he's so big. I'm smaller though and this bus is more full so a lady sits next to me. She's not fat exactly but her leg presses against mine.

"Hi," she says.

"Hi," I say.

She's shaking out candies from a little box and sucking them into her mouth. The bus goes out of Eugene and down under the highway, cutting up a slope. I can see black mountains against the dark sky ahead.

I close my eyes and there's rain on the metal roof of the bus and then it stops. Later we cross a little bridge and below the edges of the ground slip away and black trees have fallen over around stumps and far below smooth blackness. Water.

"Lake's down," the lady says, leaning across me at the window. "They let out the dam, after the summer. You traveling alone?"

"On my way home," I say.

"How old are you?"

"Seventeen," I say. "Is that candy you're eating?"

"Lozenges," she says. "Want one?"

"No thank you."

"There's so many creepy people on this bus," she says, whispering. "When I saw the seat next to you I just went for it."

"I know," I say.

"The bus is really different in the day and the night," she says.

"Darker," I say. "How old are you?"

"Forty-four," she says. "Why? I was born in Bend. I've seen it change a lot."

"What?" I say.

"The town," she says. "What part do you live in? One of the new developments?"

"No," I say, and turn away to the window and rest my head on my hand.

After a while it's been quiet and on the fogged up window I start to write my name but the lady might be watching so I add a P to the first three letters then draw a fish under them. I wipe that. I think how somewhere tonight Nameless is sniffing at the air or running on all fours or trying out his squirrel language. He's way behind us now.

I can feel the lady breathing on the back of my head and listening I can tell she's asleep. I look back and can see Father's tangled hair, his head taller than anyone's.

"The bathroom," I say, and try not to wake the lady as I step over her thick legs. She shifts and takes up more of my seat by the window but doesn't open her eyes.

Father is careful not to look at me as I come down the aisle. He looks straight ahead and maybe is pretending to sleep.

"Caroline," he says with his voice low and sharp when I sit next to him, close.

"It doesn't matter," I say. "It's dark. No one's watching."

"Everyone's always watching," he says. "That's how we have to think."

"I want to say some things," I say.

"You were talking to that lady sitting next to you."

"I believe in you," I say. "In the city I had to say those things since I was afraid. I love you and I know you are doing everything for us and that I can't always understand why."

"She is watching us," he says. "What did you tell her?"

"Nothing," I say. "She's asleep. I'm sorry."

My face is close to Father's. He smells the same as he always does. He jerks his face away and scrubs at the cloudy window and looks out.

"I'm your girl," I say. "You came back to teach me so we'd never have to be apart again."

"Stand up, Caroline," he says lower than a whisper. "Follow me and don't say anything. Be sure to get your things."

His red frame pack is stuck in the shelf above and finally he gets it loose. I follow him toward the front of the bus and when I get my pack the lady still looks asleep. My picture on the window is fogging back over but still there.

Father stands at the yellow line by the driver you're not supposed to cross.

"Excuse me, sir," Father says. "Would you let us out up here?"

"Where?" the driver says.

"Anywhere here's fine," Father says. "Our cabin is just up over that ridge there."

The bus slows but does not stop. Outside the black pines fill the windows.

"Any special stops are supposed to be cleared at the station," the driver says.

"I spoke to them about it in Vancouver," Father says. "We transferred buses, you see. Please, sir. If we go all the way to Bend, we can't get home until tomorrow, and my wife will worry about the girl."

"Please don't tell me you have luggage underneath," the driver finally says.

"No, we don't," Father says. "None at all."

———

THE WINDOWS OF THE BUS are dark. I can't see any faces looking out. The red taillights don't last long and then we're alone and it's darker all at once.

"Feels a lot colder," I say.

"It's the altitude," Father says.

"Are we close to a town?" I say.

"Not really," he says, "but look, the number on this road here looks familiar to me."

It's not a paved road, and not really gravel, just worn down dirt. It looks like a fire lane in the forest park but more overgrown.

"I have some friends who live around here," Father says. "Who have a cabin up here, somewhere."

"Where's the moon?" I say. "I thought it was out before."

"That nosy woman," he says. "She was asking you questions, wasn't she?"

"I didn't say anything," I say.

"She could have had the police waiting for us in Bend, or even in Sisters, waiting to take us back to Portland and all that. Would that have made you happy?"

"She was just a lady," I say. "She didn't care about anything but that lake. She was just a boring lady."

The road slants upward. Enough light comes down through the trees that the edges stick out. The potholes and ruts are easy to follow.

"So what are you saying?" Father says. "That I made us get off into this forest in the middle of the night for nothing?"

"No," I say. "I don't know."

"Better safe than sorry, Caroline," he says.

"I know that," I say. "You're right. So you really know where we're going?"

"It seems familiar," Father says. "That's all I said. Are you tired?"

"Not exactly," I say.

"Good," he says. "Good girl. If we slow down too much we could really get cold."

"I'm already cold," I say.

"No you're not," he says. "You just feel cold."

The road levels and the trees open up and thicken again. We pass through a stretch where we have to climb over trees fallen across the road. Some are blackened and burnt. Some of the standing trees are just sharp black spikes against the gray sky. Father is explaining about the forest fires when it begins to snow.

"Better than rain," he says.

The flakes drift slow and heavy at first. Father takes off his pack and takes out two white plastic shopping bags. He puts them over my feet with rubber bands around my ankles to hold them on. He has his boots but I have only my sneakers. I don't know when he took off his empty black eyeglasses.

Pretty soon the snow is sticking to the ground and we're walking on top of it.

"I read about igloos before," I say. "It's warm inside there even if the ice is cold somehow."

"Sleeping in the snow is a lot more fun to read about than to do," Father says. "I promise you that. Here."

He straps the headlamp across my forehead but the light only pulls snowflakes into my eyes and makes it more impossible to see. I switch off the switch without seeing anything. The wind is stronger now and the air is colder and the snow is sideways. I have my head turned a little to be able to see at all and in that moment along the edge of the road she comes running, dark against the white. It's Lala with her mouth open and there are no other dogs with her, her thin brown shape and her tail slipping past and then gone behind us.

"Lala!" I say.

"What?" Father says. "Who?"

"A dog from the forest park," I say. "She just ran past us. Didn't you see?"

"There's nothing out here," he says. "Just keep walking. Are your feet cold?"

"They were," I say. "Now I can't even feel them."

"That's good," he says. "That's a good sign, as long as you can keep walking."

"This is a slippery kind of thing to have on your feet," I say.

"Better slippery than wet. Trust me on that."

The trees open up and then close in again. It's gotten darker, it's not even lighter when we're out of the trees. I don't know if we lose the road because of the snow or before that.

"We could start a fire," I say. "No one would see it."

"Everything's too wet out here," Father says. "What would we burn?" He says something else but I can't hear it.

"What did you say?" I say.

"I don't even think we have matches," he says.

"Do you really know where we're going?" I say.

"I think so. It's been a long time." He turns all the way around and then we head in a slightly different direction. "Also," he says, "it's snowing and it's the middle of the night. That complicates matters."

If I walk close behind him it blocks some of the snow. We keep on without talking. A little later we come to a stretch where there's strips of black in the ground like roads or water so the snow stands out white like islands around them.

"Yes," Father says. "Very good." He takes off his glove and puts his bare hand on the ground. "We're in luck," he says.

"What?" I say.

"How much do you know about volcanoes?"

"Some," I say.

"There's heat inside the earth," he says, "and some places it comes up."

"Look," I say, pointing over by some trees, where there is smoke. "Someone has a fire over there."

I can feel the bottom of my feet again, warm as we run across the black rocks. When we get there though it is not a fire but a pool of hot water. Steam cooks up into the sky. The air smells like eggs. Father stares down at the water then sets down his pack. He holds his bare hand against the water. He touches the water with his finger and jerks it back out.

"Hot?" I say.

"Oh, yes," he says. "Sit down like this, here, Caroline. Stretch out."

All the ground is warm. I can feel it through my jeans, all along down my legs. Father rolls over from his back to his front, he stretches out his arms.

"These black rocks are broken up lava," he says with one in his hand. "They used to be liquid. Isn't that hard to believe?"

"Where are we going?" I say. "What are we doing?"

"If you keep asking me these questions," he says, "that really throws off my judgment."

"Sorry," I say.

"Everything will be a lot easier in the daylight," he says. "Our focus right now is just making it through the night. And that's no problem. We're lucky. This will be a night we'll remember. It's an adventure, our adventure. Hey, if we had a tarp we could make a kind of tent and catch all this heat and it would be like spending the whole night in a steam bath."

"We always have tarps," I say. "Blue ones."

"I gave them away," Father says. "I lost them."

We wait like this. We turn over and turn over again. I warm up my back until my front is cold and then the other way around. The wind blows and the snow is still falling but it melts as soon as it lands on the warm stones around us. Trees grow around the clearing and it's black beneath them. Someone standing there could easily be watching us if they could see in the dark. I am thinking of the lady on the bus and all the other people and where they are now. Bend? I wonder what we would have been doing now in Bend, where we would be spending this night.

"Are you asleep, Caroline?" Father says.

"The rocks are too hard," I say, "and half of me is always cold."

"I'm thinking of getting into the water," he says. "To raise up the temperature of the core of my body."

"Go ahead," I say.

"I think you should, too," he says. "You don't want to catch cold. Be sure to take off your watch first and put it in your pocket."

My clothes are warm and damp and heavy. The plastic bags have melted off my feet so there are just scraps held onto my ankles with the rubber bands.

"Hot!" Father says behind me, splashing.

It's been since we lived in the forest park that Father has seen my whole body and I know it's changed but he doesn't say anything and it's dark. Still the way my body looks makes me want to get under the water faster even though it's so hot like needles with only my foot in. The bottom is gravel, not sharp gravel. The pool is maybe two feet deep and not so wide. Father and I both fold our bodies around so almost everything is under. His hairy legs are pressed soft against mine. I slip deeper in the water so it makes a hot circle around my neck, rising up.

"Don't let it get in your ears," Father says.

"Why?"

"I can't remember," he says. "Something about the bacteria."

"What about all the other holes in our bodies?" I say.

"I don't know," he says. "They're farther from our brains. Doesn't this feel good, Caroline?"

It does. Where I am coldest is deep inside me and the warmth eases in a little at a time, further and further. My feet that I hadn't been able to feel before now come back to hurt. I feel a heartbeat in them and then that slows to an ache and then they feel like the rest of my body and skin. My wet hair on my neck is cold. I sink down a little to change that. I see Father through the steam and then he's gone and is back. I see the dark mark on his shoulder that is the tattoo of my name even if I can't quite read it. All he wears is his bracelets. The water is freezing in his beard so his face looks sharp like porcupine quills around his mouth.

"Is this place going to explode?" I say.

"No," Father says. "It's not an active volcano and it's too far away. It's been thousands of years at least."

"But it could," I say.

"There would be warnings," Father says. "Noises and trembling."

"Did you really not see that dog?" I say.

"No," he says. "I'm sorry I missed that."

The dark shapes of the trees are cut off by the steam too so their tops hang loose in the dark sky, the clouds from the pool. My skin is all loose, the gravel sharp against my hip. My fingers are all pruney. I listen closely and can hear the snowflakes melt I think as they hit the hot water.

"How long have we been in here?" I say.

"What?"

"Keep the water out of your ears," I say.

"I think we shouldn't stay in for too much longer," Father says.

We climb out and pull on our damp warm clothes. Father is hopping and balancing on one leg as he pulls on his pants. Steam rises up from his wet head toward the trees like his body is smoldering inside. I look above my head and see the same thing. My body feels warm deep down in the core like Father said.

We stretch out on the stones again. We don't talk. We are both awake. We turn over and then turn over again. Father melts snow by holding his plastic mug in the pool so we can drink. We eat all the almonds which are the only thing we have to eat. Three times in the night we get back into the pool and then out again and lie some more on the stones, waiting. The snow never stops falling. We're never quite dry but never quite cold.

IT'S SO MUCH EASIER to see in the morning. It's still hard to understand where we are or where we are going. I am trying not to ask Father these questions. He's standing and stretching his arms over his head.

"That wasn't so bad," he says, "was it? We'll feel a lot better once we start walking and get the kinks out."

There are no birds or squirrels or chipmunks I can see. In the white snow there is not one footprint. We walk out across a meadow and then into more blackened trees. The bark is all burned off some of them so they look like a completely different kind of tree.

"Could all this be from the volcano?" I say.

"No," Father says. "It's a forest fire. We're safe, here. Look down there, there's a river. I wonder if there's fish in it. We might be able to catch them."

"Why?"

"To eat them," he says.

"We're vegetarians," I say. "And we don't even fast on Fridays anymore."

Father stumbles since his feet break through the crust of the snow and I can walk along on top. There's one green tree surrounded by all the burned spikes and fallen blackened trunks like it's been spared or gotten lucky or been somehow stronger. It's a pine tree with the longest needles I've seen.

"Fasting works best when you're eating on the other days," Father says.

"But we'll go back to it."

"Yes," he says. "When everything is right again, yes."

Some of the burned standing trees are half gone and hollowed out, jagged sticking into the sky and when you walk around they're only an inch thick. One of these has perfect round woodpecker holes in it that look like two eyes twenty feet off the ground.

MAMMALS HAVE DEVELOPED effective ways of living. Some mammals can hibernate. Such adaptations have made mammals dominant today. Among mammals are animals that man considers the most important animals alive today. Mammals add greatly to the interest of forest, field, and desert. Man is the most adaptable of mammals.

THE CABIN IS ALL COVERED in snow so it's hard to see. It is an A frame which means it is the shape of an A, tall and pointy.

"This is it?" I say. "Your friends' house?"

"Let's see," Father says.

The door is locked. Father twists the knob and leans with his other hand and his shoulder and it cracks and splinters a little as it swings open.

"Take off your shoes, Caroline," he says. "Be careful not to track anything in."

It is darker and the kitchen is just inside the door. The refrigerator's cord is unplugged and it's open. Father turns on the faucet and nothing comes out. He kicks the small rug aside then and pulls on a ring in the floor he knows is there and then he pulls open a trapdoor and with the headlamp on he goes down there.

"Just have to turn everything on," he says with his face looking up. "It's all turned off so it won't freeze."

There's a photograph stuck to the refrigerator. A woman with red hair wears a bikini and a little girl has a thick orange life preserver strapped around her. A fat man with a mustache is the father. They stand on a dock next to a white boat and they are all smiling and squinting against the sun.

"What are their names?" I say.

"Who?" Father says.

"Your friends."

"Roy and Sylvia," he says.

"And they have a little girl?" I say.

"Probably," he says. "I haven't seen them in a while."

There is a black metal woodstove and firewood which we do not burn since we don't want to make any smoke. If we had to we would but there is a round plastic thermostat on the walls and electric baseboard heaters along the walls. Our frozen clothes are thawing and dripping so we put them in the bathtub and find blankets. There are smart secret drawers everywhere. The washer and dryer fit in the closet and are stacked on top of each other. Up a ladder is a bedroom with one big bed and one small bed. There's a clock with blinking red numbers that say 12:00 and a shelf full of books. Even if the electricity is on we don't turn on the lights. We keep the curtains closed and light candles. It is all right that we are here but we don't want to have to explain it to someone who might not understand. We keep all our things close to the door in case we have to leave quickly.

I am just happy to be getting warm with my damp socks, my

feet pressed against the smooth metal of the baseboard heaters. I look up at the sharp angle of the roof that is blocking out all the snow and wind.

Father spreads maps he's found across the table. "The thing is," he says, "I know this country pretty well. I've been around here before."

"Which is why you have friends here," I say.

"Right."

"Are we still going to Bend?" I say.

"No," Father says. He laughs. "Actually we were never going to Bend. I just bought those tickets to throw the people off."

"Which people?"

"The followers," he says.

"But we weren't planning to come here," I say.

"Not exactly," he says. "We're close, though. Tomorrow."

There's pea soup in the cupboard and also saltine crackers that are not too stale. This we eat and also macaroni and cheese even though we don't have milk or butter. Upstairs the dark green sheets are flannel and the down comforter is so warm and the bed is soft. I can't even think about last night and this is better than the hotel too which is probably all gone and in rubble now, demolished. This is better than our house on the farm since Mr. Walters isn't close and watching us and better than the forest park since no one expects us to be here.

"I wish we could stay," I say.

"Not even the people who own this place can live here all the time," Father says.

Still my toes go numb and back and forth but they are not

exactly cold. Father snores and I poke him until he rolls over. We are so tired.

FATHER FIXES THE DOORKNOB in the morning. He puts a new rubber washer in the sink's faucet. There are many ways to pay someone back and be a good friend.

When he goes down under the house to split the logs in the woodpile I have our clothes and the sheets in the washer. I'm vacuuming upstairs to make the lines in the carpet like they were.

The girl's name is Melody. It is painted, her name on the small wooden bed and also written in some of her books which are some coloring books and then some others that I recognize. They are *Golden Nature Guides: Fishes, Flowers, Birds, Whales and Other Marine Animals, Mammals*. I had all these and also *Insects* and *Fossils*, a long time ago in my bedroom in the house with my foster parents. That is a very long time ago. I carried these books around. I liked nature then but I didn't know anything about it.

I remember the *Mammals* book especially, the drawing of the animals exactly like they were before. My favorites are the ones who can change colors with the seasons so they can hide better. The snowshoe hare is white in the winter and brown in the summer. In the spring and fall it is somewhere in between.

On a piece of my scrap paper I write Thank you, Melody, and carefully trace the picture of the snowshoe hare and all his different disguises. I fold this paper and slide it between the other books where she will find it.

When the laundry is dry we make up the big bed again. My socks and underwear are still warm from the dryer. I can feel them in my pack, between my shoulders.

We are only borrowing the orange plastic sled and the snow-shoes and besides all the firewood is split and the house inside is cleaner than before. Father's snowshoes are wooden and have crosses of sinew and mine are red plastic and are actually Melody's.

We walk and walk and walk. The snowshoes are kind of heavy but they make it easier and Father isn't falling through the crust anymore. He pulls his pack and a jug of water on the orange sled which smoothes the snow behind it.

"What are these orange poles?" I say. Thin, they are sticking up through the white snow.

"This is a road," Father says, "but it's closed. They don't plow it. The road is six feet beneath us and these orange poles show where it is."

Later in the afternoon we come to a long slope. Father is in back and I'm in front between his legs on the orange plastic sled. Slow at first we push with our hands and then slide racing down. The wind is cold in my face and the white snow kicks out as we shout just missing the trees at the bottom and not stopping, leaning hard and still going with the sled skidding across icy stretches.

NONE OF THE BUILDINGS in the town of Sisters are really more than one story tall. Slush splashes up from the tires of cars and pickup trucks. Standing at the post office you can see in every direction, to the four edges of the town. I stand there next to Father who is delighted since there's two checks in the post office box he set up before we left Portland. Everything is working like he planned it to work. He deposits the checks in the Wells Fargo ATM but doesn't withdraw any money since he has plenty already.

"I'm delighted," he says. "How about we find a restaurant and eat something?"

The sun is out and the sky above is blue but there's clouds resting all along the mountains. In the window next to me stand cowboy boots with flowers painted on their sides.

"Are you limping?" Father says.

"No," I say. "I'm just used to wearing those snowshoes. Do you think we should walk together? I could cross the street."

"Let's not worry about that," he says. "Not today. I'd like to walk with you."

He takes my hand. Our snowshoes and the sled and Father's big pack are all hidden at the edge of town. All we have is my small pack so we look like regular people walking down the street. No one hardly looks at us.

It's the middle of the afternoon so not many people are eating at Bronco Billy's. Some of the furniture looks like wagon wheels and the menu says it has the best hamburger in the state of Oregon. I have a grilled cheese sandwich and tomato soup. Father has a garden burger. We share a chocolate milkshake.

"I can't believe I'm warm enough to eat this," I say.

Father's got those same maps spread out on the table while we eat. His finger traces along a crease.

"Are we staying here?" I say.

"Close by," he says.

"You still have a lot of friends here?"

"Some, maybe," he says. "People move around all the time and that was years ago."

"Before I was with you."

"Exactly," he says. "And now I feel like things are really finally changing."

"Better or worse?" I say.

"Better," Father says. "Like we could get lucky for a while. I haven't felt that way in I don't know."

"Are you still mad at me about the bus?"

"I wasn't mad, Caroline. Everything is working again," he says. "Now we just need to find a place to stay for a little while."

"Inside or outside?" I say.

"Oh, my girl," he says. "My heart."

Six

GROCERY SHOPPING ALWAYS makes me feel that something in the future days is promised or settled, that there will be the time and a place to eat the food we buy. At Ray's IGA in Sisters we get bread and peanut butter and packets of oatmeal. Matches and candles. Raisins. Apples and carrots.

We eat the bananas as we walk across the parking lot since it's hard to carry them without crushing them. The sun is down. It's fun to sneak out of town, separate from Father but keeping him in sight. We watch for headlights, hide behind trees.

When we get back to where we hid our things it's all still there. Our packs are on top of the snowshoes to stay dry and the sled is on top of it all with two branches from a pine tree pulled over it by Father to hide the orange color. No one has found it. We switch the food from the plastic grocery bags into Father's red frame pack and then we buckle on our snowshoes and start up the slope.

The day was so sunny and the sky blue but already the storm is coming when we don't need it. Neither one of us says anything about the snow as it starts out and this time it doesn't start slowly.

"We could just walk back down and hide our things again," I say. "We could get a motel room at that place near the grocery store."

"We can't afford it," Father says.

"You have all the money," I say. "And we just got those two checks from the post office."

"I mean the exposure," he says, "not the expense."

"You could get a room for yourself," I say, "and I could sneak in later."

Father stops for a moment and looks back toward the lights of town that we can still see down below.

"No," he says. "This is better. This will be better. Trust me."

The snow blows down hard and sideways and slanting. It's cold in my eyes.

"Walk behind me," Father says. "You'll get a little cover, that way."

He's pulling the sled though so I can't walk too close and the toe of my snowshoes keeps kicking it.

"Caroline," he says.

"I'm not used to how long they are," I say.

I can tell Father is checking all the houses we see in case they're empty but there's lights in the windows so far.

"It's the weekend," he says. "That's why they're out here."

"Why?"

"These are just their vacation houses," he says.

Smoke twists out of chimneys and inside people are probably sitting watching the orange fire and its sparks crackling.

"Those people don't care if anyone sees their smoke," I say.

"Yes, Caroline," Father says. "That's right."

"That would be nice," I say, and he doesn't say anything back.

We keep walking past big houses and log cabins and A-frames like the one we slept in last night even if that seems longer ago.

I know Father won't let us go back there even if we could find it. It's a long way away. Even if it was close it wouldn't matter since we couldn't see or find it.

A dog barks somewhere, the sound mostly lost in the snow. After a while I can't tell if we're walking up or downhill. The snow swirls around from every direction and blows straight up from the ground.

For a while there's the thin posts like orange fishing poles sticking up through the white snow, a curving line that we can follow one at a time since that's as far as we can see.

"Is this the same road as before?" I say.

"No," Father says. "I don't know. We'll find someplace. Don't worry. Right up ahead somewhere."

"When we left the city," I say, "you told me you would take me someplace that wasn't so cold."

My snowshoes seem heavier than his. They look like they're heavier. Even if we could hibernate I don't know where we'd go. All we have left to follow now is the poles for the electrical and telephone lines that could be stretching to a city a hundred miles away. The sled keeps dumping the packs off and I have to put them back on top.

"Are we walking in circles?" I say. "I haven't even seen the road posts for a long time. Those orange ones."

"I don't know," Father says. "I'm trying to guess where the moon should be."

WE CAN'T EVEN FOLLOW our tracks back to where we knew where we were since they are all filled in. The snow is only falling thicker. It's later and it's darker.

"Over there," I say. "Look."

"What is it?" Father says.

The little shack is almost buried in the snow. Its outside curves, rounded. Two windows glow only a little like there's something inside but not enough light to really see anything. We stand there. The snow piles up on our heads and shoulders since we aren't moving.

We walk closer next to black cords of wire that snake down off the telephone pole and down low, just above the snow to the tiny round building.

Father knocks on the wooden door three times and nothing happens. He knocks again louder. He pushes the door and it scrapes open. Snow shifts down from the roof above.

"In anybody inside?" Father says.

There is a faint glow and a buzzing sound at first.

"Yes," a voice says, then. "We are inside."

"Who?" Father says. "Sorry," he says as the headlamp lights up their faces and they squint at us. It is two people. A lady and a boy.

"We found it first," the lady says. "Close the door if you're coming in. If you're not coming in, close it, too."

Her hair is blond and wavy down past her shoulders, one side sticking up more. The boy wears a yellow and black striped cap like a bee, his face wide and pale and staring.

"Don't trip over those wires," she says as we step in.

Father closes the door and we are inside. I can't see except for the circle of light from Father's headlamp sliding along the dirty plywood floor.

"Are you a little girl?" she says to me. "We didn't expect visitors."

"We got lost in the storm," I say.

"Caroline," Father says, like he should be the one talking. "We did get a little turned around," he says to the lady.

"Is someone after you?" she says.

"Followers," I say.

"Caroline," Father says.

"Who?" she says.

"Just for tonight," Father says. "If we can share your shelter and warm up a little then we can figure things out. The weather."

Now a faint glow comes off the walls and that is the only light. The air smells like metal. Dry and baked and rusty.

"We'll be out first thing in the morning," Father says. "Is it all right with you if I light a candle?"

"Light a candle," the lady says. "You can sleep here. People have to sleep."

The cabin is only one room and there's not much place to stand. There is a bench built along the wall and the lady and the boy sit there. There are no other chairs and there's a black plastic garbage bag next to the boy where maybe their other things are. They are only wearing jeans and T-shirts and sneakers. There's one little table and a bunk bed frame that is splintered and broken without any mattresses.

The lady's name is Susan and the boy's name is Paul. The two of them haven't moved at all since we came inside. They lean against the wire that's wrapped around and around the inside of the walls, loose across the bottom of the door. It's been all stripped down to its copper. Susan: I've never seen a lady look the way this lady looks. Her white face has sharp edges and it keeps shifting like it's never quite still, alert like a squirrel in a tree. Her fingernails are painted dark and in the dim light this makes her fingers short or like they have been cut off.

"Have you eaten?" Father says. "We just bought a store of food in town."

"Town?" she says.

"Sisters," he says. "Down in the valley."

"We're fine," she says. "Thank you."

"We're fine," the boy says. His voice is as high as mine and he is my size but he isn't talking very much.

"We ate in a restaurant," I say. "It had the name Bronco Billy's."

Their eyes are half-closed as they watch us eat. We sit on the floor. We both eat a handful of raisins then an apple with peanut butter. The water is half-frozen and almost too cold to drink against my teeth.

"Who's after you?" the lady says.

"No one," Father says.

"The girl said you had followers."

"What it is," he says, "is we're just trying to be left alone, you know, to live the way we want to."

"Yes," she says. "That's not so easy. We know all about that. Someone always wants to get involved."

Father's hair is starting to stick up because of the air in the room, lifting to show his ears. I reach up to feel how mine is sticking up.

"Your hair is two different colors," the boy, Paul, says.

"We dyed it," I say. "Now it's growing back my real color."

When we finish eating there's nothing to do and not very much space. The lady and the boy do not quite have their eyes closed but they aren't saying anything.

"Caroline," Father says. "This kind of round structure is known as a yurt. We're lucky these people are here with their yurt tonight." He turns toward the lady. "At least let us sit out of the way," he says. "The two of you can stretch out to sleep."

"We like it this way," she says. "We're used to it, we're comfortable."

"You'll sleep sitting up?" Father says.

"We like it this way," the boy says.

We take out our clean socks and underwear to use as pillows beneath our heads. Father blows the candle dark and we stretch out.

In the darkness the buzz of the walls crackles in one place and then another with a little white light and then it will just relax into the buzz that is almost a hum. The wind outside whistles hard and then into a deeper kind of sound. It blows the snow like mist across the window that I am watching and then right at the window so it's like someone throwing a handful of white sand against the glass. On my side I feel Father pressed against me, between me and the lady and the boy and I can hear them breathing through their mouths and I know how they look, sitting there. I am not cold and I am not exactly warm. I am thinking that the wind sounds like a ghost and then I am thinking about the picture that Miss Jean Bauer showed me of the house in the storm and the story I told about the people inside and the people outside seeing the windows and being cold. This tonight is kind of the same as that and also kind of different but it's still almost like I could see that it would happen to us from all the way back then.

I OPEN MY EYES in the morning and I've turned over to my other side during the night. Father faces me, snoring softly and past his shoulder I can see the lady and the boy, Susan and Paul, still sitting on the benches, still leaning against the wires. She wears a thin copper strand as a necklace. He has a necklace and bracelets too. They sit watching us and my eyes are barely open so they can't even tell.

"It's a man and a girl," Paul says.

"They came last night," Susan says. Her blond hair is so thick it's almost matted. It isn't sticking up and staticky like Father's or mine that I can feel around my face. Paul still wears the striped yellow and black stocking cap.

"They're our friends?" he says.

"Yes," she says. "We're going to have a fun day."

"They came last night," he says.

Without opening my eyes wider I stretch out my hand and touch Father's neck just below his whiskers. He opens his eyes and I watch his face as he remembers where we are and smiles to see me.

"Caroline," he says. He sits up and stretches his long arms over his head and groans. "Good morning," he says to Susan and Paul. "Looks like the weather cleared some."

Outside the window it is bright white everywhere but the snow isn't falling. The sky is pale blue, hardly darker than the snow.

"We really owe you," Father says. "It was so late last night. We were in quite a predicament."

"You had to sleep somewhere," Susan says.

"Are there any outlets here?" Father says, "or just all the wires? I don't imagine you have a way to heat up water?"

"No," she says.

"Did you tap into the transformer out on the pole yourselves," he says, "or did someone else string that wire? Ingenious."

"We have water," she says.

"We have water, too," he says. "I'm just thinking about getting some breakfast together."

I sit up too. I feel a sharpness in my throat from breathing the humming dry air all night. The bread we bought at Ray's IGA isn't too crushed since it was in the top of Father's pack. With a fork we can hold slices close to the walls and toast them that way. We eat toast and apricot jam. We eat an apple and an orange. Paul and Susan just watch us.

"There's plenty," Father says. "We're happy to share."

Susan is mixing orange powder into plastic jugs of water. Paul holds one up to his mouth. It looks heavy. Bubbles rise up and he makes noises in his throat that make me thirsty.

"That's fine," she says. "We'll just drink for now. It's Tang. You and your girl should have some."

"No, thank you," Father says.

"Is it like orange juice?" I say and feel that my tongue is a little sore and swollen from where I bit it last night. "I like orange juice," I say.

"It's too sugary," Father says. "Have a little more water, Caroline."

"It's good energy," Susan says. I see her take more of the orange powder in a scoop and pop it straight into her mouth, dry like that.

When I am changing my socks the toe of the left one is black and stiff with blood. I turn away from Father but Paul sees how the top of my foot is worn down with the skin shedding off and my toes raw too.

"We've been walking and walking," I tell him. "These days we've walked all over."

"It is just so difficult not to draw attention," I hear Father say. "Once they've found you and they're interested."

"Yes," Susan says. "That's the trick. From San Francisco to here, that was a race. Staying ahead is the trick."

"It's tiring, that's for sure," Father says.

"That's a horse with numbers on it," Paul says, leaning over and looking down into my pack. "I've never seen one before," he says, "but that's what it is."

"A horse is a mammal," I say.

"What?" he says.

"You're also a mammal," I say.

"Oh."

"Mammals are warm-blooded," I tell him. "Back-boned." I pull out the book and hold it open. "Look," I say. "A rabbit is not a rodent." I show him the fox or dog family picture with the wolf and coyote and poodle at the top and the dog-like mammal that looks more like a cat and lived forty million years ago.

"Did you ever own a dog as a pet?" I say.

"A dog?" he says.

Father is sitting on the bench now with his shoulder almost

touching Susan's and she has her fingers around his wrists even though they won't reach all the way around.

"Pretty good bracelets," she says. "They must really help you."

"Maybe," he says. "Could be the placebo effect."

"They're good ones," she says again. "Pure copper. I can tell. What's this? Are they tarnished?"

"We were in a hot springs the other night," Father says. "It's probably the minerals in the water or something."

"We spent a whole night in a hot springs," I tell Paul. "We kept getting in and out of the water so we wouldn't freeze to death."

He listens to me and I can't tell how much he even hears. I understand then that what makes it so hard to talk to him is that his face hardly makes any expressions and his voice doesn't hardly rise or fall when he does say something even if maybe he is just copying the way Susan talks. Also, he has no eyebrows.

"Don't you have anything to show me?" I say. "Where are you from? What are you carrying?"

"Caroline," Father says, overhearing, stopping me. "How about the two of you go outside for a little while?"

"Yes," Susan says. "We adults have to talk. There are some things we have to figure out and decide."

"I thought we were leaving first thing in the morning," I say.

"Caroline," Father says. "You could go sledding or something."

My shoes are still damp. I am thinking not to trust these people since I don't understand them and Father and I are fine by ourselves. Father sees something in them to trust, I can tell. He's not even looking at me as I scrape the door open.

Outside there's no sun but brightness comes from every direction out of the snow. The orange sled is frozen down where we left it so I kick it loose with my good foot. Paul just watches me, still wearing only his jeans and his T-shirt.

"Aren't you cold?" I say.

"Cold?" he says.

"You can borrow my jacket, if you want it."

"Sled," he says.

I reach out then and take hold of the striped cap and pull it off his head and drop it on the ground. His head is completely smooth without any hair at all. I can see the blue veins between his skin and his skull. He's not mad and doesn't say anything, he just bends down and picks up the cap and shakes the snow out of it and puts it back on.

"What happened to your hair?" I say.

"We don't have hair," he says. "That's all right, to not have hair."

"Who?" I say. "What is your problem?"

He is fast, already climbing up the slope. I step in his footsteps and pull the sled behind. The way the light is it feels like it's already afternoon and I can't tell by my watch how long we slept or what time of day it is.

From the top of the hill we can see the edge of the yurt's roof, some of the snow blown off. I think of Father and Susan inside there now. Talking and looking at maps and planning and maybe doing other things I don't know.

"You two are not like us," I say. "Just because we're all out here like this and there are two of us and two of you."

"Sledding," Paul says. "We're sledding, right?"

"Are you thirteen?" I say. "That's my age."

He sits in front and holds on to my legs and then I go in front. It's faster if we put the sled in the same path as before where it gets worn down and icy. We scream and laugh and fall off the sled at the bottom so it gets away into the air and bounces off trees. We keep doing it again and again.

He is breathing harder, now he's the one who can't keep up when we're climbing to the top. He never pulls the sled behind him. I wait there at the top.

"What do you think they're doing in there?" I say.

"Who?" he says.

"In the yurt," I say. "The adults. My father and your mother."

"My mother?" he says. "She's not my mother."

"Where's your mother?" I say.

"I don't know," Paul says. "That's all right not to know that."

His jeans and T-shirt are completely wet and crusted with ice but he's not shivering or anything. Next to us is a shallow puddle and both of us are reflected twice, once in the ice and another reflection balanced on the head of the first, a shadow on the snowy hillside.

"My mother is dead," I say.

He just points down at the sled. "We could try it with you on your front," he says, "lying down flat and I could lie on top of you."

"You're as big as I am," I say. "Why should you be on top?"

This time I'm in front and we're going faster than before.

Halfway down Paul's not holding on enough and he falls off and I hang on. I just scream. At the bottom I look back and can't see him.

"Hey!" I shout. "Paul!" But he doesn't answer.

I'm pulling the sled back up the hill when the lady's voice starts. First I hear it and next I see Susan standing outside the yurt holding something red. She sets it down to hold her hands up to her mouth to shout louder.

"Paul!" she shouts. "You come down here now! Leon! Paul! Stanley! Paul!"

While I watch and listen Paul is plowing down through the snow toward her without making any noise so I see his head rise up into where I'm looking and then his body standing down there close to hers.

When I reach them she's already buckled my red plastic snowshoes onto his feet.

"Those are mine," I say. "What are you doing?"

"I worked it out with your father," she says. "This red pack, too." She is wearing Father's snowshoes buckled tight to her sneakers. She looks different than before since her hair is now straight and black but then I see that it's that she's wearing a black wig on top so the blond hair shows out one side.

"What is happening?" I say.

"We traded," she says. "It's all right, dear."

Paul lifts one snowshoe then the other. He looks up at me.

"We were sledding," he says.

"Away from here, now," Susan says. "It was very nice to meet you. Goodbye."

"Goodbye," I say.

"It was very nice to meet you," Paul says and then they are walking away with the snowshoes making scratching sounds in the snow. He is not as fast and stumbling, learning to walk in those things. She has Father's red frame pack on her back and her head looks too tall with both those wigs.

I push the door of the yurt scraping open. The air smells like burnt plastic and worse. I can hardly breathe. I turn my face to the open door for a moment before I can go inside.

"Father?" I say.

All I can tell is that the wires are torn loose from one wall. None of them are glowing any more at all and it is hard to see since there's not much light from the window. I kick the head-lamp and then find it and shine it across our scattered things and then see the edge of Father's shirt. I shine it up and across him and right to his face. His teeth are biting together and his lips are pulled open. All his hair is burnt down close on one side and his beard is not hair I see but blackened burned skin. I cannot see his ear on that side very well.

"Father," I say. "Don't worry. Rest."

He jerks once and kicks his leg then like sometimes he does when he's asleep and then he doesn't move again. There is no breath, no heartbeat in his throat. If I ran after Susan and Paul I might not catch them and if I did they wouldn't help me since she is the one who did this to him. The town is down the valley, Father said last night, so if I keep going down I'll find it. Sisters. If I go alone, can I find my way back to him? Will I get back too late?

I try to move Father and can't. He's not snared up in the wires, he's just so heavy. I've always been proud of how big he is. The best thing I can do is open the door and kick snow inside, and then put the orange sled on top of that. I roll Father and pull him out the door and then I can see him better.

All the buttons and snaps and zippers of his clothes are broken or gone. His hair is breaking off like ashes against the snow. Around his throat there's black burnt lines heading beneath his undershirt. His right sleeve is gone and that arm is black and red with the sharp white bones at the elbow. That hand is so burnt it doesn't look like a hand. His left boot has been blown all the way off even if his bare foot looks fine. I find the boot inside and it's shredded and useless. Instead I put one of his wool socks on that foot. It's then that I see the sole of his foot is all blackened with a hole in the middle.

"Hey!" I shout, standing and turning in a circle.

It's getting darker. With the headlamp on even in that small space I have to find everything one at a time and my clothes and papers are all scattered too. I'm coughing. I fit everything and Randy and our food which they took none of into my small pack with the broken zipper.

Now that I don't have them I see how much help the snowshoes were. Still, the snow has frozen a hard crust that I can walk on top of but Father's weight on the sled keeps breaking through and I have to strain harder. He slips halfway off. His head catches the snow and holds and the sled slips out from under him. Shifting him up it feels like his one arm is just loose and only held on by the sleeve of his shirt.

It's impossible to go uphill and going sideways is not easy and the deep hollows around the trees try to pull the sled in.

Downhill it's hard to keep control and really the only way I can go. Only downhill is toward the town of Sisters and now I am not so sure that it's a good idea to go there.

"I don't know what to say," I say. "I don't know what to do. You're the one who taught me everything."

And I know as soon as I say that that he did teach me everything, that even if Father is burnt up and not talking, he would say, "Caroline, think. You are the sharpest girl. You like a challenge and anything you can handle. Think, Caroline."

A STALACTITE FORMS FROM dripping water on the stone ceiling of a cave. Usually limestone, but this can also happen in lava caves. Where the stalactite drips on the cave floor a stalagmite may form. Where the two meet, if they do, this is called a column. It takes a long time for them to form. Deep in its cave, a stalactite has surprising beauty.

IT'S BEEN HOURS since I saw the sun. The air around me is darker but I'm also under the thick pine trees where the deep holes around the trees pull at the sled and I have to be careful not to walk too close to them. I don't use the headlamp unless I have to. Father's really too wide for the sled and his good arm keeps falling and dragging behind above his head like he's waving at the sky.

First I hear engines. I look up but there are no helicopters, there's no chopping in the air. The sky is clear black and the stars are all across it, the Dipper upside down and the Milky Way. The wind blows snow out of the branches, down at my face.

And then there's headlights down below and coming in pairs, zigzagging their way upward and coming closer. I am not afraid. Father would not be proud if I was afraid.

The headlights stop and the engines rattle down and I hear car doors slamming. It's not long before there is shouting, voices. I slide the sled down under the cover of a fallen branch, careful not to let the sharp needles poke Father's face. He is hidden. My shoulders hurt as I step away and my hands from where they held the rope. I feel lighter, floating since it's so easy to walk.

I'm in the trees hidden and a flashlight jerks up the slope, one bright circle switching back and forth. The people are just dark shapes coming closer. There are three of them, then four even though it seems like twice as many since the moon is out now and the black shadows against the snow make it look like every one is two.

The first one is out ahead and now he turns and shouts back: "Up here! The cave's right here, the opening!"

"The mouth!" one of the others shouts and they laugh.

Down below more headlights come close and wink out. More dark shapes stumble and laugh upward sometimes with flashlights and sometimes just following the trail broken by the first people. I watch. I wait. I think of Father, cold and hidden nearby beneath the branch and the cold snow beneath him through the thin plastic of the sled.

Staying in the trees I climb closer to where the man said the cave was. I see light, flickering light from a fire. There's voices of men and women and loud music with drums.

"There you are!" a man says, off to one side of me where I wasn't looking. "Trisha!"

Closer, he is almost my age, almost a boy.

"No," I say. "I just."

"What are you doing out here?" he says. "I thought you were Trisha. Was just draining the main vein, you know, but it was like pissing an icicle, you know? Freeze to death. Your name's Helen, right?"

"Right," I say.

"So you came up with Carter and them. Cool."

"Yes," I say.

"Let's get back to that fire," he says.

It's so loud inside the cave. Everyone is shouting and a boombox is playing music of more shouting. There's twenty or thirty people and the cave could hold more probably. Everyone is young like teenagers and only a couple older. Some of them are wearing puffy camouflage coats and snowmobile boots like they're going hunting. Others have on ski pants with racing stripes and matching jackets and gloves that have zippers on their backs. The air smells like dirt, like smoke, and the floor of the cave is hard dirt with stones in it.

I drift away from the man and closer to the fire where mostly boards and splintered posts are burning. Sharp nails stick black and hot out of almost everything. Cigarettes are smoked down, passed around, flicked into the fire. Tall shadows of the people climb up on the walls and ceiling, through the smoky air. It seems like they all go to school together and I think it's a high school but maybe they're a little older. They like to shout and jostle each other, pretending to fight.

A boy hands me a red plastic cup. I sniff at it and it's bitter. I pretend to sip at it.

"I love beer," he says.

"Yes," I say. I say cheers and hit my cup against other people's cups when they say it to me. Mostly I stand by the fire. When someone stands up from a log I sit down.

My left foot hurts and then it doesn't hurt. The ceiling stretches twenty feet above and slants down on the other side toward the back. The stone up there is black like there's been fires here before and the black stretches in a thick line across to the mouth of the cave which is where the smoke escapes. There, at the mouth, someone is trying to drag in a small pine tree or a broken off branch and someone else yells that it's too green and covered in snow to ever burn. For a moment I worry that the branch was taken off Father, but no one says anything like this and still I think of Father out there waiting for me to return and guarding my pack where there is food. I'm hungry now but there's nothing to eat in the cave.

"It's so cool," says a boy next to me. "Tons more fun than if we were in someone's house or a condo or something. No one's parents would ever have a clue. My dad would shit, if he knew where I was."

When I look over at this boy I see he's really just talking at the fire and not looking at me or expecting me to say anything. He's wearing a ski mask so I can only see his puffy chapped lips and his bloodshot brown eyes. No one is hardly bothering me. They just keep drinking and shouting. My face is hot and my back is cold. I turn around and watch two boys who are trying to crawl as far back in the cave as they can. The firelight flashes on the soles of their boots. The ceiling slopes down there and there's just jagged black spaces stretching back.

"Son of a bitch!" one boy yells.

"Motherfucker!" yells the other.

The cave swallows up their voices and doesn't really echo.

"Rad hair," a girl says, sitting next to me. She has a sharp chin and a striped hat on her head. Her face flickers.

"Thanks," I say. "I think there's bats that live in this cave, probably."

"What?" she says. There's a pompom made of yarn on top of her hat.

"Bats probably don't like all this racket," I say.

"I know you from chemistry," she says. "Right? I didn't know you partied."

"Chemistry," I say. "I think so."

"God, I'm thinking of dropping that class. Were you at Mary's party last week?" she says and then looks past me at three boys coming close.

"Keg stand!" they yell, pointing, and then she's over by the metal barrel and they're holding her upside down while she drinks beer from the black hose.

I keep having these conversations that are not quite conversations. Mostly I am trying to stay close to the fire and to wait for the night to be over. I keep thinking if someone I talk to seems like a friend or a person I could trust that maybe they could help us but no one seems like that. They are only getting drunker and more stupid.

A girl vomits and someone puts snow on top of it. A boy across the fire from me stands and unzips his pants and takes his penis out and pees on the fire with a sizzling sound. He almost falls over, sitting down. Someone behind me is saying that lava came through this cave, a long time ago, that that's how it was made. The batteries on the boombox are wearing out so the music goes wobbly. Words are just stretched out sounds. No one seems to notice.

I just stare and stare into the red and yellow and orange flames. After a while I look up and there are maybe only ten people left in the cave. A tall boy in a ski parka with a beard and snowmobile boots comes over to the fire and looks at the few of us that are left sitting there.

"Keg's kicked," he says. "Now or never, everyone's taking off."

"We should put out the fire," a girl says and then everyone says that doesn't matter, that it's not like the cave would burn down.

"What about all this leftover wood?" a boy says. "I carried it all the way up here, man, but I'm not carrying it down."

"Next time, maybe," another boy says, "or whatever."

I stand and walk outside, where the moon is even brighter. The air is freezing cold in my nostrils and throat but is fresh and thin. I cough and taste smoke.

"Did anyone get Jared?" someone says. "He passed out, before."

"Yeah," someone else says. "They dragged him through the snow and that woke his ass up!"

"Helen," the tall boy says, and it takes a minute to tell that he's talking to me so I turn around.

"What?" I say.

"You got a ride with Courtney, right? I think she's waiting down there. You can get a ride with me or Jericho, though." He points back toward the cave.

"Tell Courtney I'll ride with Jericho," I say.

"You sure?" he says. "All right."

He turns away down the slope and I wait and then follow a little. I check back and no one else is coming out of the cave yet so I drift over to the side, into the trees. I hide while people start coming out and stumble past. Below cars are driving away with their red taillights going smaller.

I wait. No one calls and no one comes back. It's quiet again with the moonlight and at the mouth of the cave some orange flickers and glows.

Only once I get closer do I think that animals could have found Father there and licked and bitten at his bloody hand or pulled at the bones showing in his arm but when I take the branch away he's there like he was. He stares up at the sky. His hair's burned off and his beard and there's frost on his face.

"They were having a party in the cave," I say. "They're all gone but there's still a fire."

The sled has frozen a little to the ground and I kick Father's side by mistake getting it loose. Then I put on my pack and carefully slide him down through the trees out at an angle across the slope. In front of the cave the snow is stamped down by all the footprints which makes it easier to pull the sled. The ground inside is frozen near the mouth so I pull until the sled catches on the gritty floor and then I drop the rope.

The fire is mostly coals so I drag over some boards and pile them on, careful of the nails. I blow on the coals and sparks snap up and bounce across the cave's floor. It is still hours until the morning and there's nothing to do except to wait and try to stay warm. I'm not hungry anymore even if now I have the pack.

Somewhere Susan and Paul have Father's pack and our things. I think of them walking away with our snowshoes and wonder how far they got and if they're inside somewhere and maybe thinking of us now. I don't know why they did what they did and left us or why they didn't want to be with me and Father. Perhaps it was all an accident, but we don't believe in accidents we simply adjust the way we're going.

The fire eats away at the wood. I stare into it for a long time. A thick board buckles and gives way and everything collapses so the places the flames lick all change. I stand, I add wood. I stare. I am thinking of how Father came after me and how he found me, how I didn't even recognize him or know who he was when I first saw him.

That was in Boise Idaho when we're all planting trees all around in our neighborhood even at people's houses who aren't in our ward. My foster father is wiping off his bald head and laughing. The trees will grow to shade our street.

That day Father is dressed in a blue dress shirt and his hair is cut as short as it was after they caught us and kept us in the building, before the farm. That day with the trees he looks like anyone's father but he doesn't have any children with him. Even then he doesn't tell me who he is right at first. I just think he's a friendly man from the next ward over and the strongest person there. He can pick up the small trees with their bundles of roots by himself when it usually takes three people. He tells me once that he likes my shoes, that I'm a pretty girl. He thanks me for holding a shovel.

While I'm sitting next to the fire in the cave and remembering all this it's like Father has rolled over a little in the sled and is watching me from twenty feet away. His eyes shine against the fire and he knows what I'm thinking. He cannot say, "Don't look backward now," he cannot tell me not to remember.

Now I stand and walk back toward the mouth of the cave where he is waiting with his eyes still open. His mouth looks like he thinks all this is almost funny. His arms are stiff like frozen and hard to move so I can reach into the pockets of his jacket and his pants.

These are the things that I find and take from Father: his small notebook full of writings, two wooden yellow pencils, over four hundred dollars in a plastic sandwich bag, the three sharp knives and the long scissors in their oilskin case, his seven copper bracelets. These round bracelets are too large and slide over my hands too easily but still I put them on my wrists. The sound of their clinking is like Father is helping me to do all this now as I try to move him from where he is.

"You made a mistake," I tell him. "It's not the fault of Paul and Susan but your fault for liking them and thinking she was the same as you when she was different than us. It was a misunderstanding and you thought it was an understanding."

I kick in snow and bring more in. Some of it breaks off in slabs and I throw them down in front of the sled and slide it this way deeper into the cave, back to where the ceiling slants down and ends and the floor drops away. Father is heavy but from the pile of wood I take a thick board and wedge it under him. I lift so he rolls out of the sled and off the edge. He lands with a solid dull sound and even when I stick my head into the darkness I can't see where he is. I don't say I'm sorry since he knows why I'm doing this and that there is always a way not to draw attention when one does not want to get caught. There is always time to think about one's feelings after the necessary actions have been completed.

I breathe in hard, one time, and am careful not to hit my head on the shelf of rock above as I pull myself back out. I drag the board over to the fire and throw it on and sparks leap up. I get more wood than before and keep piling it on until the fire has a roar, a wind of its own inside it. I get warmer. I let myself get hot. It is easier to remember, now.

I am not even ten years old yet, back in Boise. It's a warm night when it happens so my sister Della and I are sleeping out on the round black trampoline in my foster parents' backyard. Our sleeping bags zip together and we're in nightgowns so it's plenty warm. She is asleep and the lights are out when Father comes silently over the fence. He stands so still and calm next to the trampoline with his giant hand around a silver spring. I remember him from the ward tree planting, how much everyone liked him.

"I'm sorry it took me this long," he says. "I've come for you, my daughter."

"What?" I say. "My father's inside."

"They adopted you," he says. "Temporarily. They're good people but they have to give you up. If you look deep inside you'll feel that you truly aren't theirs, and that they aren't yours. Come on, now. Gather up your things. These larger shoes on the ground here are yours? That's right. Put them on."

"Can I say goodbye?" I say.

"I wish it could be like that," he says. "Right now we don't have time."

"What about Della?" I say.

"Don't wake her."

We don't climb the fence. We go right through the gate and out the driveway and walk past the dark houses of all the people in the ward, houses where my friends are sleeping. A car passes and does not slow down. We're in no rush. I'm afraid and excited at the same time. I keep thinking we'll go back and then I think of what he said and I do feel something. The calm and sure way he said it all makes me believe and see how this has been coming without me even seeing it.

In the foothills not far from new houses being built Father has a camp. Deep in thick bushes he's dug a kind of cave into a hillside with a roof that slants over so it's hidden and hard to see. It's like an earlier copy of our house in the forest park and not nearly so nice. That's where we stay that first night. It takes me a long time to fall asleep and Father does not sleep at all. He watches me.

In the morning we eat bread and peanut butter. Father wears dark jeans and a green sweatshirt.

"I'm so happy," he says. "Aren't you happy? We're together at last. Finally. I've missed you so much."

Later we hear searchers, people close by calling my name. If I answer they will take me away from him and he says bad things will happen to my sister and my foster parents, to me and even to him. He knows things about them, about everyone. We sit silently. The searchers call my name, then it's silent, then they pass in the other direction. We eat more bread, more peanut butter.

"What's kind of funny," Father says, "is that name they're calling isn't even your real name. You know that, right?"

The next morning he leaves me there in the camp in the hills outside of Boise. He puts on the blue dress shirt and all the clothes so he looks like an elder from the ward. He shaves and combs his hair with water. Even not standing next to other people he is I think the biggest man I have seen.

"I'll be back," he says and I tell him to wait, that I can come along, but still he makes it so I can't go anywhere, so I can only move a little bit.

That day I hear more calling and I sit silently by myself. I shift my legs under me. I stay in the shade. I squint at the sun and watch the line of shadow move along the ground. When Father comes back it's almost dark.

"Where did you go?" I say.

"To search for you," he says. "I joined a search party."

"But you know where I am," I say.

"So they wouldn't be suspicious," he says, and unlocks my hand. He starts to unpack some food he's brought in a plastic bag.

"I don't know," I say. "I don't know if you're really my father."

"I understand that it's confusing," he says. "We had to give you up. Your mother was ill and when she passed away I couldn't care for you. It was temporary. You see that."

"My mother?" I say.

"You and I are together now," he says. "That's what matters, here. Things will start getting better from right now, but I need your help."

"What about Della?" I say.

"Who?"

"My sister."

"Oh," he says. "Yes. I don't know her by that name. We won't forget her, we'll be back for her. We just have to wait for things to settle a little bit before we go after her. Right now I can only take care of one daughter. Aren't I taking care of you?"

He unfolds a piece of newspaper that has my picture on it, and my sister's and my foster parents'. He lets me read the article before he takes it back.

"They aren't bad people," he says, "but they have to let you go, they have misunderstood things." He lights a match and burns the newspaper away. "If I weren't your father," he says, "how could I have walked right into your backyard and walked away with you and no one said a word? It was the right thing to do, it made things right, and that fact is why we're together, why you knew better than to cry out or draw attention. I need you to be brave, Caroline."

"All right," I say.

There is something fun and something scary in these first days when we're getting to know each other again. Already I am dressed like a boy with a knit cap and blue jeans and sneakers. I wear a football jersey Father gave me that has the number 55 on the front and on the back. Sometimes we stay in the shelter in the hills and sometimes even in the city. We never sleep on the streets or at the homeless shelter but sometimes Father finds a friend like the clerk from the Boise Co-op who has a small apartment with a couch and records. I am not to say a word when we stay there.

It's all like Father says since out in the open it's so clear how things are. I walk past posters with my face on them, my old name, and no one sees me. I see people I know from the ward, and the rule is that they have to call out and recognize me first before I can say anything to them and they never do. Sometimes they're close enough to reach out and touch. People tie blue ribbons in the tree branches for me since they think that is my favorite color even if my favorite color is yellow. I read about the blue ribbons in the newspaper. Father reaches high and pulls one loose for me and I fold it up in my pocket to keep.

"My heart," he says, "from now on it's best if you don't speak of your foster parents or your sister, to me or to anyone. If you can keep from thinking about them, that would be best. It will get easier."

These days are only practice for who we'll be and where we'll go. We're not staying in Boise, we're heading west since already Father can see the future and how we'll live in the forest park, all the happy days ahead.

Seven

THE FUNNY THING IS THAT the city of Boise has grown and spread out everywhere and still Father's camp and shelter are hidden and it looks like hardly anyone has ever come through the underbrush and found it. There's a couple bent beer cans in the back and that's all.

That's where I stay the first night I get to Boise. There's still the flat stone where the stove went, the one shelf that held the pots and pans, even the metal pipe with concrete on both ends like a barbell too heavy for almost anyone to lift. The scratches of the handcuff are still on that pipe where it slid back and forth when I was left alone.

Sitting here now I wish in a way that it was back then and we were here together. We could set out and do it all over, every part except the end even if that was meant to happen. Even if it was and it happened again I'd like to go back to right here with Father, starting out. I would try to help Father not to make the mistake he made by thinking the lady and boy were like we are. I am angry at Father even if he couldn't help it since now we are apart and I am alone.

To get here this time was easy. Mostly since I had the money though there's less of that now. It was afternoon by the time I walked into Sisters and I found the bus station without asking anyone.

This is the day before yesterday: I pretend when I get on the bus that I'm with the lady in front of me and there's lots of room on the bus so I don't have to sit next to anyone. I lie down with my arm looped through my backpack and fall right asleep. Everything about me smells like smoke from the fire in the cave.

It's sunny when I sit up and we're almost in Boise. I can tell by the shape of the mountains and I don't need a map to find my way around. I don't need to ask for directions.

First I buy a new sleeping bag that costs almost one hundred dollars. Second I buy two pairs of wool socks, third some batteries and then a blue stocking cap that says GO BRONCOS in orange knitting around it. That's the name of the sports teams at the university.

Then I buy nuts and bread and fruit and water, as much as I can carry. I am not worried about anyone recognizing me. If they couldn't see me before when I was with Father and looked the same as they remember they'll never see me now that I'm taller and dressed this way with my pack and all my hair up in the cap. I limp but am not slow. It's a long walk and confusing since so much has changed and there's so many new houses and none of the new streets are straight, up in the foothills. There's yellow machines parked where flat parts have been cut into hills, and houses half built where I could stay but I will not stay. Finally I understand and I backtrack some, I am careful like someone is following me even if no one is. It's almost dark when I reach the end of the houses, up high where there's snow on the ground. There's dark paths beaten down through the snow from people or animals or both. That's the way I go.

Up at the top of the slope I know where I am. Looking down

I see the yellow squares of light that are windows and the flickering televisions and the snap of darkness that means someone is going to bed. Caroline, I am thinking. Smart girl, no one knows you've come back.

I circle around some before I find it and then I carefully take out the headlamp and keep it pointed down. The ground is not too hard and I unroll my new sleeping bag. My left foot is blistered up. It's not easy to move the toes but it doesn't hurt as much so it's getting better. I almost build a fire to dry out my shoes even if it would draw attention. The truth is that my feet have grown and I should have bought new shoes especially for the weather but I did not since I was trying to save Father's money.

I burrow my cold face down. It is a mummy bag that goes down to ten degrees and it can be zipped from the inside or the outside. I use up the end of the old batteries in the headlamp reading about mammals and then reading some of what Father wrote to keep in his notebook. Sometimes I have to take out the dictionary to look up his words. Before I put the headlamp away I load it up with new batteries that I bought in case I need it in the middle of the night.

Coyotes I hear crying out but I am not afraid of them since they are intelligent animals who eat mostly rodents, insects and fruit.

EVERY PROBLEM I HAVE comes from believing something to be true that is not true.

IN THE MORNING it has snowed and the hawks slide back and forth across the sky like they don't know where to go. I slept straight through to dawn with my hat on and I pull it down tighter. It's too cold to get up without going somewhere and too early to go anywhere that I need to go. I read some more even if it's hard to turn the pages with gloves on my hands. Then I fall asleep again and it's later in the day when I wake up.

The sun comes in bright but low and cold. I keep feeling that a wind is about to start up and it never comes but there must have been wind since most of the snow is blown away from the ground around the camp. Snow would make it harder to come and go, I would leave footprints.

My shoes are even tighter with the new wool socks. The sky is darker now so I carry everything with me as I head out to see what I can find and to do what I came here to do.

It's also funny to walk down the hills and onto the streets, back along through the neighborhood in the opposite direction but the same path as Father and I took that night when Della and I were sleeping on the trampoline. Walking now I keep expecting his shadow or the sound of his boots on the blacktop next to me. Still he could see how all this would happen and is trusting in me so it's not exactly like he's not here.

I pass the white brick wardhouse with its spire and all the rooms I know are in there. The big kitchen, the room full of folding metal chairs that can pinch your fingers, the basketball court, all the hymnbooks whose songs I know.

Dogs bark from behind wooden fences where I can't see them. Only their paws below or their snouts sticking through. Dogs bark from inside houses, standing on couches so their noses smear against the windows. I go past the old penitentiary, through Quarry View Park, slanting along toward Hill View, the street I'm after.

None of this feels like a place I've lived, not like I'm coming home. I'm on the sidewalk like a boy from another neighborhood with my GO BRONCOS cap and my backpack.

The trees we planted have grown up, at least two feet some of them though right now they have no leaves and look skinny. One day they'll be tall and strong enough to climb. It's been so long since I climbed a tree.

A new part has been built onto the top of my foster parents' house. It used to be yellow and now it's blue but it's the same house. The white car in the driveway is not our red stationwagon even if they could have gotten a different car, a new car. It could even be that they don't live in this house anymore which is fine if this is true since it was never my plan to ring the doorbell or to come back and be their daughter. It would be fine too if they knew how I turned out and were proud. They are not bad people even if the things they believe are unbelievable. They tried to hold on to me longer than they were supposed to, to make me be like them when I am not like them and have places to go.

I only wanted to walk past the house like this to show that I can and that it doesn't make me feel any special way. After all they are not the person I'm after.

IF ONE ADVANCES CONFIDENTLY in the direction of his dreams, he will meet with success unexpected in common hours. He will pass an invisible boundary. Don't forget this. Don't forget that thinking can get in the way. Forget the forgetting. We seek to forget ourselves, to be surprised and to do something without knowing how or why. The way of life is wonderful. It is by abandonment.

I WENT TO ADAMS SCHOOL all the way up to fourth grade. The brick is the same soft orange color as always and behind the school is the swimming pool that is hardly ever open and when it is the water is so cold you can't stand it. There's a twisting green plastic slide called the Hydrotube that you can see through. In the wading pool there are concrete sea lions you can climb on. Now like usually the water is drained and the gates are locked and there's no one in there.

I keep walking. Out in this playground I played four square and tetherball and soccer. I climbed these monkey bars and hung upside down so my hair swept the black rubbery ground. Now I wouldn't even go to this school anymore. I'd be in middle school, almost high school.

Where I'm standing I can see blackboards through the windows and sometimes a person's head, a teacher. I could probably remember the teachers' names. I know some of them are still here since some of the cars in the parking lot are the same: the tan and cream Suburban of Miss Larsen, the PE teacher's fancy red Jeep.

When the school bell rings you can hear it outside, across all the fields and all through the neighborhood.

At first all the tiny kids come out with bread bags sticking out the tops of their rubber boots and their mittens attached together with a piece of yarn stretched inside their coats and down the sleeves.

Then I see her, surrounded. Della. Her brown hair is lighter than it used to be and now she has curls that she never had before. She is ten years old and surrounded by laughing friends. She is taller than she was. I always was skinnier. Her books pressed into her chest, she shouts at some boys climbing a fence. Della is pretty, she was always prettier than me and followed the rules. They said I could learn from her, watch her. Still I wasn't a bad example when I was here and then I was gone. Now I am back and she can learn from me.

She talks to her friends next to the yellow school bus. When they get on she does not get on. Instead she watches the bus drive away with her friends waving in the windows and then she crosses the street and begins to walk.

A whole flock of little black birds keeps rising from the branches of one bare tree to settle in another for a moment before something startles them and they rise up and return to the first tree again. I am thirty feet from my sister, though she is walking away. I follow. I am not afraid, I am only trying to time it right. I want her to hear me and not be frightened. I want to tell her my new, real name. Little sister, I want to say, I know so much more now and I've come back to take you with me to be my friend. I can teach you. This where you are is not a bad place and these are not bad people but it's not where you're supposed to be. It is not who you're supposed to be with.

I follow on one side and she's on the other side of the street. I want to see her better but I can't seem to cross over and there are parked cars so I can only see her head sliding along. Her face never did look like mine, her earlobes attach differently. I used to wonder and ask Father if maybe our foster parents had gotten us separately and he says, "Oh, Caroline, you two are sisters. Don't be jealous like that. You'll always be my first girl now."

Now I can see Della's whole body, walking, and we are the only two people walking on this block with just the width of the slushy street between us. She doesn't look over at me. It's like she doesn't want to or doesn't recognize me or is afraid. I take off my stocking cap so my long two-colored hair is down but she doesn't know who I am. I almost wave and I almost call out her name but I do not. It's not since I'm afraid, afraid she won't remember. It's more that I don't want to wave, that I don't want her to remember. I see that now. I wanted to see her without being seen even if the plan has always been to come back for her with Father, the three of us. Now without him I don't know. I do know that I am not the same sister she had.

This girl across the street, her name is still Della. She smiles and laughs to herself as she walks like she's remembering something that happened at school or thinking ahead to where she is going. Her black shiny shoes slip a little on the icy sidewalk. She's not even in the same day as I am even if once we were sisters and shared a room. There's a way that I think she should know it's me if she's really my sister. To just feel that I am near, or to tell by how I walk or move that it's me. She even glances over across at me and then glances away. Nothing. I know I am not that same girl and now I really feel that and know that Father knew better than I did when we left her here, behind.

THE PIONEER CEMETERY is down Warm Springs from the elementary school and is surrounded by a black metal fence but the gate is not locked and swings open. I walk along the spaces between the headstones and not on the paths. I used to get in trouble for playing here during recess. Some of the stone crosses and angels and even the names are familiar. Some have settled into the ground and stand up crooked. That's a sad thing to see. Some have sunken down so far the grass is growing over.

There's footprints all around some graves but most of the graves are surrounded only by the white snow, smooth since no one has visited. Do dead people need their family to visit them or is it sometimes the other way around? Who gets lonelier?

There is a place here that I remember, that is under some tall trees where the parents of my foster parents are buried and where we sometimes took flowers. There's spaces there waiting for my foster parents and for Della and also for me even if that's a place I'll never be.

As I walk closer to this place I see that there are new stones. Maybe my foster parents have died while I was gone and then I think that maybe they gave up on me after I disappeared and they could not find me. I am thinking that maybe they even put up a stone for me with the ground beneath it empty and not dug up at all. I want to stand there by my stone with no body beneath my feet since the name carved into the stone would be the same name I wrote once on a slip of paper and put into the hole of Randy's stomach, to remind me of a name I will never forget but that I will never use again.

Under the trees though I cannot find the names I expected at all or the stones that I know. I brush off snow, I kick it off the names that are flat along the ground. This is not the right place or the graves have been moved around. No one's here. My feet are wet and cold again. The sky is getting darker. I walk to every cluster of trees and do the same thing but never find the names I thought I would find. It really doesn't matter, I hardly know why I'm searching. Finally I cross out the other side of the cemetery, past the little black birds that hop along the snow's crust without making any mark.

And then I see what I forgot, that East Middle School is right across the street from the cemetery and inside are the people my age who I knew and who I do not want to see now. I see instead a bus coming and I wave to the driver, feeling in my pockets for coins.

RABBITS AND RODENTS are both mammals but a rabbit is not a rodent. They are part of a different family. A family is a fundamental social group typically consisting of a man and woman and their offspring. It can also be two or more people who share goals and values, have long term commitments to each other, and usually reside in the same dwelling place. Families are also a way like species and orders to organize how all kinds of animals are related to each other. A father is the male parent of an animal. Most animals have nervous systems, sense organs, and specialized modes of locomotion, and are adapted for securing, ingesting, and digesting food.

ON MY RIDE I DON'T see any blue ribbons on tree branches or car antennas or pinned to peoples' clothes. I have changed so much and learned so much it's like everyone is moving slower than I am and I can tell what they'll do next or even what they are thinking. Yes I'm sad to be alone but it's fun too or at least satisfying to see all that I can do for myself.

When I see the shopping mall I pull the cord and climb down. I'm crossing the parking lot and my shadow is long and thin, slanting away with my head rounded by the stocking cap. Then the black shadow of a crow slides along the pavement next to me, across me. It squawks and bends straight up a brick wall. I look into the sky and there's nothing there.

Fluorescent lights are not healthy for you and they are everywhere in the mall. I've been here before though and it's warm inside and the crowds make it safe, the open spaces that are not inside any store where people ask if they can help you. No one keeps track of you at the mall.

Mervyn's, J. C. Penney's, Mrs. Fields Cookies. They have stores of everything: caramel corn, teddy bears, jewelry, sunglasses. A fountain out in the middle where people throw coins into the water. Near there stands a tall fake candy cane and a throne and a sign for Santa Claus. He's not there. Christmas is almost a month away but the music is playing in the air.

I turn around. No one is looking at me even if it feels that way.

I have forgotten to eat, which is a mistake. Everything around me is a corn dog or hamburger. A&W Root Beer, McDonald's, Taco Time. I take three toothpicks of cheese from Pepperidge Farm, dig nuts out of the bag in my backpack. My legs are tired since my pack is heavy. The sleeping bag is light and rolls down small but there's also all the papers and Randy and the mammals book, Father's notebook and knives, the dictionary and the food. I want to set it down for a while so I sit down on a bench with it on the floor. I take out an apple and eat it while people walk past not looking at me.

Across from where I'm sitting is a sewing store and in the window fabric is all unrolled and hanging. One long piece is dark blue with yellow and orange birds swooping across it and squirrels down along the bottom. I almost forget my pack when I stand up to look closer.

The smallest piece of fabric I can buy is a yard which costs ten dollars. The lady who tells me this has thick eyeglasses and a measuring tape over the shoulders of her brown cardigan sweater.

"What are you making?" she says.

"I don't know," I say. The truth is I saw it and it made me happy.

"All right," she says. "Will there be anything else?"

"No," I say.

Once I watch her cutting the fabric and the silver scissors going through it I have another idea.

WITH THE FABRIC FOLDED in tissue paper inside my pack I go down the long back hallway until I find the women's restroom. I wash my face and in the stall I hang my coat. The stall door is made of steel and has initials and curse words scratched into it.

I wet the bottom of my T-shirt and back in the stall wipe it over myself and put on a clean shirt. The one I was wearing smells like smoke. Later I will change my underwear but first I take off my cap and wet my hair down. It smells like smoke too and the water brings out the smell. In my pack I find my broken off half of a comb and comb my hair straight down past my shoulders. The faucet is automatic when I put my hand there which is hard to learn and keeps starting and stopping.

There's mirrors on two walls at the corner of the sinks so I can see the front and side of my head at the same time. With my coat off Father's bracelets clink around my wrists so I take them off and stack them on the counter. I take his long sharp scissors from the oilskin case and it's easier to cut the left side of my hair than the right where I have to turn my hand upside down and can't exactly see the blades cutting. The bleached part of my hair goes from my ears down and my regular black hair is above. The line between them is uneven and a little blurry and that's what I follow. My hair will be all black again, just like it always was back in the forest park.

First I hear the door and then in the mirror I see the two girls coming in and standing behind me. One has red hair and freckles and is tall and the other shorter girl has blond hair. The first thing I do is take Father's bracelets off the counter and put them back on my wrist. These girls are about my age and they both wear headphones whose cords come out of a Walkman in the short girl's hand. They take off the headphones so they're not attached together but don't move apart or go into the stalls. They just stand there watching.

"What?" I say. "What is your problem?"

They step back a little without leaving.

"We saw you out in the mall," the tall girl says. "We followed you. At first because we thought you were a cute boy but then you went into the women's room so we wondered."

"I wanted you to think that," I say. "I knew you were following me."

We're talking to each other in the mirror. I haven't turned around. Our voices are loud with all that tile.

"She means," the short blond girl says, "that you could be a cute girl, too."

"I don't care what you think," I say.

"I was only trying to say something nice," she says.

"That's fake," I say.

For a while I keep cutting my hair and the girls keep watching me without saying anything. Then in the reflection I see the tall girl point at the floor:

"Look," she says. "This is bad. You're hurt."

"I'm fine," I say and I don't look down since it might be a trick and I don't want them to think I'll look where they say. Also I'm right at the tricky back part of my hair. I snip around to connect the lines of the right and left sides and then with my hand I sweep the cut hair off the counter and into the sink. I scoop it up to throw in the trash can.

When I look to pick up the hair on the floor I see what they were saying. There's smeared red on the yellow and tan tiles, blood tracked all around in the tread of my sneakers. It's red footprints walking over each other. The front of my left sneaker is red and wet.

I try not to let my face show anything. The girls just stand there still watching.

"You're hurt."

"So what?" I say.

"Go get Mom," the short one says. "Right away."

The tall girl is gone, the door slapping.

"I'm fine by myself," I say even if now I don't feel fine. I pick up my pack and set it back down since it feels so heavy. I close my eyes for a moment and open them. The girl has stepped closer without me noticing.

"You're sisters?" I say.

"Yeah," she says. "Don't worry, we're going to help you."

"I could go if I wanted," I say. "I could get right by you."

"Are you crying?" she says. "Don't cry."

"I'm not crying," I say.

"Don't," she says, but she doesn't touch me and I'm past her, out the door.

I turn right and not left, not back to the mall but out the emergency exit so an alarm starts ringing. The scissors are still in my hand and the sun is bright. I slip away slow between all the cars in the parking lot, my footsteps silent and holding my breath. When I carefully look up across and over the cars no one is following. I am already thinking what to do next.

Eight

THESE DAYS I HAVE a mountain bicycle with nubbed rubber tires that can make it up and down the muddy gravel road. It's all downhill from where I live on Wildwing Road to the library so it only takes about half an hour. Under the tall trees, in and out of the ruts. I have neighbors up here who raise llamas and others who raise dogs that are half wolf. This means there must be at least one wolf with them who teaches all the dogs to howl like that. When they start in at night I think of Lala and wonder if I really saw her back in the snow and how far a dog can run and how old a dog can get. Late at night I also think of Nameless and the decisions he made and wonder if he's still trying and he's gotten further or has given up or has been caught or maybe has become a different kind of animal who can't communicate at all. I wonder where he came from that made him become like that and whether he remembers it, if he had parents or a family, whether he is trying to forget it or whether he has truly forgotten it.

All I want to tell is about Father and me but how I came out of it and how I put it together starts to become part of the story too.

That day after the mall in Boise I am afraid people will follow me, that those girls know I was there, so I catch the bus back and downtown I find a bank with an ATM on an outside wall. I take the card Father gave me and I close my eyes and remember the right numbers and where they are on Randy's body. I withdraw forty dollars and can see the balance of what Father left me which is plenty and surprising. But when I withdraw the money I see that the balance counts down and I'm thinking and thinking.

I go to the Greyhound station and buy another ticket, round trip so people will expect me to come back. Then I ride, back the way I came.

As soon as I'm in Sisters I go to the post office and I can see through the little glass window that there are two checks in our box. I write Father's name and the account number on the back of them and walk over to an ATM and deposit them right into the account. That's how I still do it, every month.

In those early days I make plenty of acquaintances. I never ask or answer too many questions. I rent a room one week at a time and I check the bulletin boards in the post office and the coffee shop to find other possibilities.

I spend a lot of time in the Sisters library which is a nice new building with even a gas fireplace at one end by the magazines with soft chairs around it. The library has a whole section of computers where people come in to use the Internet. There's a special room for children with the little chairs and tables and a few toys. A quilt of the Cat in the Hat. A mural that shows Dorothy from *The Wizard of Oz* and some camels and a bearded father reading a book to a girl.

The head librarian is named Peg. She becomes an acquaintance of mine, and then a kind of friend. She never asks questions about where I came from but only about what I want to do and where I want to go. She's the one who finds the books and explains to me how to get my GED. This takes me one year of studying and tests. Now I am enrolled in library science classes at the community college, riding the bus to Bend twice a week. It's a school where the students are all sorts of ages, so no one worries about me. People thought I was eighteen back when I was fifteen and now almost two more years have passed.

I know the Dewey Decimal System and the Library of Congress, both. I like all the colored spines of the books pressed in their shelves, thick with words. The whispering, the silence, the sound of a page being turned. I started out volunteering, shelving and reading story time for the children, and then Peg hired me as an assistant. I work three or four days a week.

At the end of my shift I take my jacket and backpack out of the office. I check out a few books to myself. I unlock my bicycle from the rack outside.

Riding through town, I pass Bronco Billy's and I pass Ray's IGA and they remind me of the times before. When I am inside them, whenever I shop for groceries I expect Father to still be there walking down the aisle smiling with a jar of peanut butter in his hand, pointing me toward the apples.

Past Ray's I turn along the McKenzie Highway where it passes all the churches: Catholic, LDS, the Community Church, whatever that means. I've never been inside them, never plan to. There's the high school, home of the Outlaws with these kids revving the engines of their pickup trucks who are my age I know even if that feels impossible. A boy yells after me and I don't look back. Even closer to my house is the middle school with its bright metal roof and its octagonal front, its sports fields out back.

I cross over and go left onto Edgington, past where elk graze

in someone's field with the metal wheels of the irrigation line.
The asphalt beneath me turns to gravel, to mud. I pass the llamas
with their woolly necks, hear the wolf dogs start to bark and
howl.

Out here there's hardly any houses, just huge white satel-
lite dishes hidden in the trees that tell you there's someone back
there. The long snakes my bicycle's tires make are the only
marks in the snow for days. It can get too deep over the last half
mile and I have to get off and push the rest of the way.

Mr. Hoffman's place on Wildwood Road is a big old log barn
turned into a fancy house with a swooping red roof. Deer and
elk antlers hang above the doorways, along the walls outside.
Mr. Hoffman has never shot anything. He buys the antlers just
like he bought the shiny taxidermied salmon that hangs over the
fireplace inside.

He is a fat old rich man from Salem who has no wife and
two grown children who never come around, which is about as
often as he does. The rooms in his house are crowded with puffy
leather furniture and dusty bronze statues of cougars and horses.
In every room there's a television and I switch them on and walk
around with all the voices going in a kind of conversation. I collect his mail which is mostly catalogs. I open the empty drawers and the mothballs roll hard, bouncing inside. I switch on his
CB radio and hear distant voices talking in numbers and lost in
static. I never push the button to say anything back. Instead I
check the water lines, the light switches, I spring his mousetraps
with a straightened wire hanger.

I am the caretaker and what I do is up to me. If I wanted
to turn on all the electric heaters and live here, he would never

notice. I could sleep on one of the soft beds in the guest room, I could cook on his shining stove.

Standing in his kitchen I look out to where the land slopes and fifty yards away in the trees I can just see the roof of my little yurt, its round window in the top like an eye staring up. Lying flat in bed I can see the stars and sometimes the moon or an airplane, a black bird zipping by. In windstorms the sharp tips of pine trees lean in.

The trees grow thick since it's the Deschutes National Forest all around us. I can run straight from my door, lose hours out there by myself in alone time. In winter I wear white clothes, in summer brown and tan. In hunting season you're supposed to wear orange so the hunters won't mistake you but I never wear orange. I blend in. I can still walk without leaving a trace. I can hold perfectly motionless and I can sway slightly, keeping pace with the trees and bushes in the wind.

The dirt is black, volcanic, sharp underfoot. Still I go barefoot when I can, when the weather allows. I wander now more than I truly run since in the week after Boise my left foot, my toes got worse. Frostbite. I read about it, how it works, ice crystals between the cells as my skin went white and waxy and then red and itchy. Frostbite can turn to gangrene, where your tissue dies away and you can lose your body piece by piece. My little toe was black and loosened already, snagged in my sock. I iced that toe down but still it hardly hurt when I took Father's sharp knife and cut it straight through. The bone made the smallest sound. This changed my balance and it's tricky to run so sometimes I wonder if I cut off the little toe on my right foot I'd get my balance back and be able to run straight again.

Just over a mile from my yurt I've dug down into the edge of a ridge and I've built a roof that hangs over further, just like in the forest park with dirt on top and a mattress inside, a cooking stove, a pine branch that leans against the front door so no one would know it's here. I hardly ever sleep here but I can with my sleeping bag and in the night I wake up and pretend that Father is next to me, that in the morning we'll walk down through the trees and across the St. Johns Bridge to the Safeway.

Lying on the mattress in the afternoon I watch eagles circle in, and red tail hawks and peregrine falcons, the egrets with their legs bent back. I've seen helicopters glide across the treetops with their noses pointing down, spilling great bags of water to put out forest fires.

Wandering and ranging I cross in and out of the burnt sections where the fires have been. Even where the fires have not been the trees here are not as good for climbing. I am heavier now but still I'll spend an afternoon thirty feet off the ground stretched out on a branch watching everything that passes below. I see deer and rabbits and elk. I hear marmots whistle to each other, see them disappear into rock piles. I've never seen another person out here. I sit in the branches without moving and animals pass right beneath me without sensing a thing so I could drop down on them like a wolverine, which is the largest weasel, a mammal that will fall from above to break a deer's spine. There are no wolverines here since now they hardly live anyplace except Canada.

A bird shouldn't be able to fly backward but I see this. Clouds come apart and pull themselves back together if I am patient enough. A red fox leaps forward three times then bounds back to where she started, her feet hitting the ground in just the same places and then coming forward again and bounding past where I can see. I sit still. A deer rattles past with its white tail coming first and its antlers dragging the air behind before it suddenly leaps forward on the same tracks. A leaf falls off the tree then raises up and reattaches itself. The sun jerks up a few inches before easing down again toward the evening.

I feel like myself with the sage and pine in my nose and all the little scratches on my bare arms. I wander across the slopes of the Black and Belknap craters, those old volcanoes, or north, crossing the highway near the Cold Springs campground where sometimes there are bright domed tents and the smell of bacon frying.

I know where the Cold Springs come up, and the Four Mile Springs, I cross Bluegrass Butte and Graham Butte, Five Mile and Six Mile. I know the names but I know buttes and springs that have no names. I follow the paths of animals, I recognize broken trees and burnt out stretches, rock formations that I give my own names. I pause above Black Butte Ranch, the bright green of the golf course and the carts scuttling across it. Out on their little lake the canoes and paddleboats drift and slide.

I come down this slope, not far from the fancy condos, the hot tubs and tennis courts and everything else. I can double back the way I came or come out on the Santiam Highway and walk back to Sisters this way, where the work crews in their orange suits are always stacking the firewood cut from the fallen trees and the burnt ones that have been cut so they won't fall on passing cars. I wave, I wonder if it's possible that some of these criminals could be the same men from the forest park, even if they got out in Portland and committed another crime and were caught again and put to work in another orange outfit.

It's miles to walk to Sisters from here. That's no problem. I cut across north of town to get over to the McKenzie Highway, near the junior high school where if there's a carnival or a softball game I slow down.

Along the dugout I like to watch the gangly girls, the ones who are fast but not quite coordinated. I can dress young, I can talk to these girls, I lean against the chainlink fence. The parents sit up high in the bleachers to cheer and shout and they think I am a friend or a sister.

There's a girl or two who seem curious, who listen and don't turn away. They pick at their cleats, they pull up their baseball socks to their knees. Lately it's the third baseman, the girl with braces and a sharp face and her brown hair in two thick braids. She's yelling at the batter to swing and the girls in the dugout are chanting about the belly-itcher.

"I played third base," I say with my fingers hooked around the sharp fence. I keep my voice low. "I was the only one who could throw it to first in time," I say. "How are you? Happy? Do you think differently than most people? Do you wonder if there's another way to live? I was a girl like you and I can tell you, I can show you."

These girls are always moving: to warm up, to bat, to field, to cheer the other team, to get in their parents' cars and drive away with their ponytails and baseball caps visible through the windows. I see my third baseman heading home with her father, his hairy arm over her shoulder, his gold watch on his wrist and sometimes I don't know if I'll have another father, another family beyond those I've had. Sometimes people ask about boyfriends or if I will ever have children and perhaps that is possible, children are. When I think of boys or men I think of Father and I don't see anyone like him around.

I do see these girls and still I wonder if any of them would understand, if one would come with me and wander and would sleep on the mattress in the shelter out in the wilderness. I don't know what a girl would think if she were sitting here with me inside my yurt where there's no windows except the round one in the roof full of sky and stars and birds slipping past, here where it takes your eyes a while to adjust. The blue square of fabric with its own birds hangs on the seventh wall and most days it seems like another window even if it is only cloth. Here the flames in the woodstove reflect in the gold letters on my encyclopedias, lined up all around the walls.

The yurt has eight walls so it is a small octagon fourteen feet across and not really a yurt at all since a proper yurt is round. I call it that to remind me of Father and how I lost him, where.

What would a girl think of all my piles of paper and artifacts from all the times, how I have broken it down to organize my story and be able to tell it? All the loose pages of my journal, my homework, pieces of Father's journal. Some piles of paper are shorter and then there's others like the first one, the pages in the forest park when I had more time and a place to write and things I wanted to say. I was happiest then, I am always trying to get back to how I felt then. It's funny how my handwriting has actually gotten worse. My spelling's always been pretty dependable.

Everything in here reminds me of something else. I have

broken all the pages into eight piles, one for every wall. They go clockwise: the happy days in the forest park, getting caught and put in the building, living on the farm, living on the streets of the city, escaping down through the snow, losing Father in the cave, Boise, and finally the eighth wall where I am now, where there is not much to say except how I am putting it together and where I am doing this.

"Valor consists in the power of self-recovery," Father writes, even if really he has copied this out of another book. I know now that some of the things he said he took from books, and so much of his writing is copying and writing back at what he copied. The three-named men are his favorites: Ralph Waldo Emerson, Henry David Thoreau, Jean-Jacques Rousseau. I am reading my way through some of these books now.

Here's another thing he copied out: "The great man is he who in the midst of the crowd keeps with perfect sweetness the independence of solitude." To this Father writes his own thought: "To be great is to keep sweetness."

Sometimes I add what I think too, like a kind of conversation. Below that I write: "How about the girl who doesn't feel alone when she is alone?"

I remember the conversations as best as I can. If I make up words he says at least they're close or taken from his notebook. I stitch it together and I only add what I have to. If I don't remember something I skip over it and leave it out. There's times like the second part where the police or Miss Jean Bauer could have taken some of my journal but even then I can't remember anything more so I don't worry too much. I take one wall at a time into my backpack and I type it into the computer at the library. I save it on a disk and erase it from the computer. Now I am near the end.

For so long I carried everything I owned around with me from place to place. Now I do have a radio, one that plays cassette tapes. And at the second wall I have the cassette tape that Miss Jean Bauer gave me of the two of us talking. She's explaining the test and then I am telling the stories of the pictures on the cards. It is strange to listen now to my little voice. I can hear how she is nervous even when back then I didn't hear that at all. She is worried about me. I am telling about the strange house in the storm and the people inside or out, the glowing windows, the story that is some of the possibilities that I came to pass through.

Father: I'm no longer angry with him for the mistake he made. He was afraid and he lost his sweetness and I could have helped him more to advance confidently in the direction of his dreams and to not confuse a misunderstanding with an understanding so he would not believe people are like us when they are not. I forgive him, I understand him. I learn mostly from how he lived his life and also from how he stopped living it.

Father and I are a family of writers. My sister Della I don't know about or about my mother even if I wouldn't be surprised to hear that they wrote too. I have always, I have sometimes imagined that I have written all this to my mother, just to show her what's happened to me and that I've turned out all right. If she were alive I would track her down and read it to her, but since she's dead maybe she's watched it all or can think what I'm thinking as I write it down. She's watched it happen and then she's seen each letter and word scratched on a page and now this final typing.

When I look back through all these times, all the girls I've been, I just laugh. Only Randy really knows, has seen it all. Randy, he moves from wall to wall, wherever he wants to go. The pebble from the forest park and the scrap of paper with the name I'll never use, they rattle inside his body. He's beat up, dirt ground into him so his organs are all one color. The 114 numbers are worn away, only slight marks where the red dots were. I remember the numbers, where they went, all the counting and mathematics I did on them, all the things I thought they meant. They did mean those things, if I thought so. Still, since then I found a book and learned that what Randy is about is acupuncture, from Chinese medicine, the places to stick needles into a horse to treat an injury or illness. For overexertion or congestion of the lungs, the point is called Hsieh-tang and is number 16, two needles stuck into each side of the nose. Number 114 is named Wei-chien, one needle only at the tip of the tail to fight heatstroke and the common cold.

How nice it would be to stick a needle in your neck or hand or elbow to treat a sadness or to bring back a memory, to be able to run faster, to make people recognize you as a friend and to understand what kind of person you are.

Here's something else Father copied into his notebook: "Every man supposes himself not to be fully understood. The last chamber, the last closet, he must feel was never opened."

There is no one to report Father missing except me. I miss him but he is not exactly missing. Out walking I search and search and I find caves and go inside them. I ask around even at school if people know about parties in caves and they say, "Caroline, we don't need a cave." Still I am out there in the hot summer and in the cold months when the snakes wait half-numb and stiff in the paths for the sun to thaw them. I range and wander. I find caves and take ropes to them, lanterns and flashlights to walk through the damp lava tubes as wide as a hallway in a shopping mall that then tighten down to where I can hardly squeeze through. Then they open up again, wide and echoing. I hear water. Bats hang leathery, complain as I pass. I don't call his name, I'll know when he's close.

Winds blow underground. They lead you to new openings, they show you the sky, suddenly bluer and brighter than you remembered.

I know my way around this wilderness. I know the landmarks on a map and I know my own landmarks. Still so often I will find the dark slot of a cave one morning and go home for water and rope only to return in the afternoon to find the cave gone, no longer where I left it.

I believe that there is movement always beneath the surface of the ground. The hollow spaces that are caves drift beneath us, carrying with them whatever they hold. A cave will sometimes meet another cave and merge with it for a time and then pass on through. The burrows of snakes and moles are taken in, their walls gone to air, the little animals dropping surprised to the cave floor. Trees' roots grasp at nothing, anxious until the dirt returns.

Caves drift smoothly beneath us without any sound. Father is missing, he is not missing. He is beyond the reach of snow and sunlight. He stays close to me, following where I cannot see but can only sense him in that darkness below. In the soles of my bare feet I can feel him say my name.

Acknowledgments

The author wishes to thank Adrienne Brodeur over and over again. Jim Rutman, emphatically. Tina Pohlman, then and now. Everyone at Harcourt, for the risk and the work. Deep thanks for time and space to Caldera and to Reed College. A debt to the amazing girls who made this story possible: Opal Whiteley, Elizabeth Smart, Caroline X. And Ella Vining, always.

From Byron, Austen and Darwin
to some of the most acclaimed and original
contemporary writing, John Murray takes pride in
bringing you powerful, prizewinning, absorbing
and provocative books that will entertain you
today and become the classics of tomorrow.

We put a lot of time and passion into what we
publish and how we publish it, and we'd like to
hear what you think.

Be part of John Murray – share your views with us at:

www.johnmurray.co.uk

 johnmurraybooks

 @johnmurrays

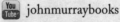 johnmurraybooks